SEX AND THE STRANGER

A Collection of Casual Fun
A Mischief Collection of Erotica

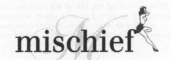

mischief

Mischief
An imprint of HarperCollins*Publishers*
77–85 Fulham Palace Road,
Hammersmith, London W6 8JB

www.mischiefbooks.com

A Paperback Original 2013

First published in Great Britain in ebook format by
HarperCollins*Publishers* 2012

A catalogue record for this book is
available from the British Library

ISBN-13: 9780007553105

CONTENTS

Contents

Picnic Itch
Valerie Grey

I married my husband, Steven, ten years ago, when I was just nineteen. He developed bad drinking habits as he moved up the corporate food chain. It wasn't going out with the boys twice a week that bothered me – it was when it became four times. I tried to get him to cut back, even going so far as to join a health club so we could work out together, but he gave up after a couple of weeks on the treadmill and consoled himself with as much booze as he could find.

I'm no nympho who wants sex five or ten times a day but when it became only once a week with my husband Steve, then maybe once a month, I began to get restless. I started noticing other men and wondered what they would be like in bed. I still loved my husband and never acted on my impulses.

I was tempted.

And then there was my husband's company picnic. It was an annual event that the employees' families were invited to, which meant at least four hundred people would be attending, gobbling food and slurping beer and plastic cup cocktails. It was at a park that had a size-able lake, leaving plenty of space for everyone to mingle without feeling fenced in.

I was feeling particularly horny that day and dressed in a pair of shorts that were a size too small and a skimpy halter-top. Underneath I wore an even smaller bikini in the hopes that Steve might get turned on and I'd get a little action before the picnic.

Steve didn't even seem to notice as we hopped in the car and drove off.

The day was sunny and a touch on the hot side and as soon as we arrived we started mingling with the others. Steve introduced me to a couple of guys I hadn't met before. Oscar had recently been assigned to work under my husband, and Hank was the supervisor for most of the trainees. Both of them were about our age and in good shape. I hit it off with them instantly, and soon we were chatting away like old friends. I learned they were married, but their wives hadn't come. Steve excused himself to go to the restroom, leaving me alone with the two guys.

I'm a born flirt and, left to my own devices, I fell into my old pattern with these handsome men. They responded in kind and soon we were having a good time trading sexual innuendos.

Steve returned and insisted on tracking down some of his closer friends. Reluctantly, I said farewell to the guys and followed my husband. The flirting had made me even hornier, so I asked Steve if we could go back to the car for a quickie. He laughed at the idea and told me to relax and enjoy the picnic.

I tried; he failed.

It didn't take long to locate his friends and drinking buddies he hung out with after work. I had met them several times and found them obnoxious. I didn't have much in common with their wives either. I was reduced to standing around and forced to make polite conversation while the guys laughed it up and slugged down beers like they were back in the college frat house.

The president of the company gave his obligatory inspirational speech that lasted a long thirty minutes and told everyone to have fun. It didn't take long for my husband and his buddies to entrench themselves near the open bar and see who could drink the most vodka tonics in the shortest amount of time. I couldn't take any more of this and asked Steve if it would be all right if I walked around for a bit. He gave a short 'sure' with a dismissive shrug that made me want to scratch his flesh bloody, and returned to getting drunk and laughing too loudly with the boys.

It didn't take long for Oscar to notice I was alone. He could tell I wasn't having a good time and asked me what was wrong. When I told him about my husband and how I felt I was being totally ignored, he sympathised and invited me to join a volleyball game that was about to start. That sounded like fun. I agreed and followed him to where they were setting up the net. Hank was there, as were three younger guys who were introduced as Ron, Todd, and Jack, all interns Hank was in charge of. The opposing team was a group of computer programmers.

'So we stand a chance, especially with you on our side,' Oscar said.

I was the only woman there and I quickly found myself the focus of a healthy amount of attention. The interns treaded carefully and didn't flirt as much. Jack was a bit raunchy. I guess they didn't want to risk saying something wrong and angering the wife of a superior. Hank and Oscar more than made up for it by showering me with very flattering compliments.

I hadn't been treated this well in years.

Our opponents arrived and the game began. I'm a very competitive woman and it wasn't long before I worked up a sweat. With a touch of flourish, I shed my halter-top and showed off my skimpy bikini. That little move made me the centre of attention of all the guys. The interns became a lot more talkative, and Oscar and Hank were

4

flirting constantly. It puffed up my ego to know I could still catch the eye of so many men.

It was a hard-fought game. We emerged victorious and I loved winning.

We were all a sweaty mess. Hank asked if I had worn the matching bottoms to the bikini and, when I said I had, he suggested we take a dip in the lake to cool ourselves off. I told him I had to let Steve know, but that I'd probably be around in a few minutes.

I returned to my husband and it was obvious he was well on his way to getting smashed drunk and showed no signs of stopping. I told him how the game went, but all he did was grunt 'That's nice,' and took another drink. When I told him I wanted to go swimming, he just waved his hand. The casual dismissal really got me steamed. He could have at least acted as if he wanted me around.

I spotted Hank and Oscar. They were already in the lake, out far enough that the water was almost up to their necks. They waved me over. I shed my shorts and ran into the water and waded up to them. They said they were glad I came by and complimented me on my bikini. Their behaviour, which was the exact opposite of my husband's, cheered me up and made me feel appreciated. I reciprocated by complimenting them on their own trunks, which showed off their athletic bodies. They returned the favour by praising my own figure.

There were few people in the water and none of them were nearby, giving us some measure of privacy. Out of earshot of anyone else, the talk became suggestive and there was a lot of sexual tension between us. Oscar positioned himself beside me as I talked with Hank. I discovered why he'd moved when I felt his hand on my bottom.

I've had guys make passes at me before and I'd always politely rejected them, but the instant I felt Oscar make contact I knew this time was different. I had never been this aroused or with two men this handsome. Rather than removing the hand, I allowed it to remain there. Taking my lack of protest as encouragement, Oscar began rubbing my bottom. In response, I moved back into his grasp. After a minute or so of groping he slipped his hand under my bikini and *really* started fondling me. I stopped talking and closed my eyes. It must have been the silence or the looks on our faces that made Hank pick up on what was happening underwater. He joined in, grabbing my breasts below the surface of the water. He played roughly with them, tweaking my nipples through the material of the top, then moved close enough to reach behind me and loosened the tie around my back. The top remained tied around my neck and the rest floated upwards, allowing him unrestricted access to my flesh. Oscar, not wanting to be shown up, slipped a hand down my front and began fingering my pussy.

I couldn't believe I was letting them do this to me, especially with people standing just several yards away, but no one seemed to notice. It helped that the guys played it cool, talking with each other casually while they worked me over with their hands. They were convincing actors. Me, I should have known better. This could create the kind of gossip and scandal that could harm my husband's career. But I could not get myself to tell these two men no. No was not on the agenda. Yes filled my money-maker and my crotch. It is during these sorts of fleeting moments of sexual wanting that people often get in trouble and spend the rest of their lives saying, 'I'm sorry, I don't know what came over me, I'm not like that.' And this was true: I am not the kind of woman who would allow two strangers, two men I just met, to touch me this way. And it was the fact I wasn't *that kind of woman* that made it more of a turn-on; it was easy to forget I was married, to forget who I was, and simply give in to this sordid passion.

Needless to say, it didn't take long for them to bring me to climax. It wasn't a big one. If anything, it left me wanting more. Hank whispered that he knew an out-of-the-way area in the park where we could continue things in private. I knew I should have refused, but due to how handsome the guys were and how neglected my husband made me feel, I couldn't even manage a token protest.

The hell with it! Why not?

7

They gave me directions, then got out of the water and headed off for the rendezvous point using a different route. I waited ten minutes, each minute feeling like an hour, before emerging from the water and putting my clothes back on. I headed straight into the woods, growing more excited with each step. After a long walk through some overgrown trails, I finally came upon a small picnic area that had seen better days. Hank and Oscar were there, waiting anxiously or so their expressions told me. Hank said this was an older part of the park that almost no one used. Given the distance travelled and that the area was heavily wooded, I was certain we'd have all the privacy needed.

I came into arm's reach and the two men were all over me. After a moment's hesitation, I was doing the same. Within seconds they had me completely naked. Oscar stopped stripping me long enough to grab a blanket he had brought and threw it on top of one of the tables. Hank lifted me up and sat me on the edge, then pushed me on my back. As he sat down in front of me, I couldn't help feeling like a meal being served. He pried my legs apart, and began eating me out like he hadn't tasted pussy in years.

I writhed on the table and Oscar leaned over and started sucking on my breasts. I'd never had two guys before; I was sorry I had never tried it. Having a tongue buried in my pussy and my breasts sucked on simultaneously made me climax faster than I had in months. Hank kept a hold of my squirming legs as he continued lapping away through the orgasm, starting me on the way to another.

Oscar stopped working on my breasts and told Hank he wanted a taste. Hank let him take over between my legs, but instead of switching over to my breasts, he repositioned me so I was lying diagonally on the table with my head over the side. I was about to protest when he dropped his shorts and allowed his cock to spring free right in front of my face. I opened my mouth, beckoning him with my tongue. He grabbed the sides of my head and jammed half his cock down my throat. When it was obvious I wasn't going to choke, he began face-fucking me in a way my husband never had. Despite the rough way my mouth was being treated, I was able to handle all of Hank's average-sized cock.

It didn't take long for me to have another orgasm but I couldn't cry out with a cock buried in my throat. Unlike Hank, Oscar stopped eating me out as I came. I began to wonder if he was going to switch with Hank again when I felt my legs lifted over Oscar's shoulders and his cock nestling itself against my pussy. Oscar jammed his entire length into me with one thrust. While he wasn't as long as my husband, he was wider and I definitely felt stretched open by the rough way he took me. He hammered away as hard and as fast as he could. I hadn't had an intense fucking like this in years, and even I was surprised by how quickly I loosened up so he could really slam away. I could feel his ball-sack slapping against my ass with each thrust. Hank stopped pumping and left his cock buried in my throat. I felt his rod twitch a split second before he began spewing his seed. It tasted good and I savoured the flavour of a man other than my husband on my tongue. It is a curious thing how every man's semen can taste different, just like they say no one vagina is like another. Hank was a healthy man. He ate healthy and his semen tasted healthy, unlike Steve's which had an alcohol and steak flavour. I couldn't remember the taste of any men I knew before Steve, and there hadn't been that many, three or four maybe, but I knew they were all different too.

Oscar was decent enough to pause while his friend came in my mouth. Once Hank removed himself, he picked up right where he left off. I came around his cock a second time, which sent him over the edge and he erupted in my pussy. Now I had the sperm of two men that weren't my husband in me and, rather than feeling shame, I was aroused and wanted more.

Oscar pulled out and Hank was up and ready again. He rolled me over so I was lying on my stomach with my feet on the ground and my bottom at just the right height for him to mount me. He had no problem plunging all the way in and started to pound me as hard as Oscar had.

I had forgotten how great a hard fuck could be.

Oscar got on the table and waved his cock in my face. I opened my mouth and leaned forward to take it in, but he pulled back at the last second. He thrust forward again, but when I tried to suck it, he pulled away and said, '*Damn*, woman. You really want this, don't you?'

'My husband hardly every fucks me any more,' I confessed.

Hank said, 'Shit, if my wife was as hot as you, I'd be fucking her every day, every hour, every second, twenty-four seven.' As if to prove his point, he picked up speed.

Oscar continued teasing me with his meat, leaving it just out of reach of my mouth. 'You really are a cock-starved slut, aren't you?' he said.

I was ready to admit to anything if it meant wrapping my lips around that hunk of meat. 'Yes. Now give this cock-craving slut something to suck on!' It was a turn-on to call myself that, to be that.

He laughed and said, sincerely, 'We'll give you all the cock you can handle.' He finally got close enough for me to suck him down, which I did with relish. Getting done at both ends was something else.

They lasted much longer this time around, Hank fucking me through another series of orgasms. I hadn't come this much in years. But even he couldn't last forever and finally shot inside of me. As soon as he was finished he pulled out and I felt empty inside. I was about to beg Oscar to take over from Hank when I felt a pair of hands on my hips and a hard prick shoved into my cunt. Confused, I released the cock in my mouth and turned around to see, to my amazement, *Jack*. He had a firm grip on my hips as he picked up where Hank had left off. He wasn't the only one either; next to him were his fellow interns, Todd and Ron, who were already naked and pointing their hard-ons at me like guided missiles waiting for the final launch codes to destroy something – my pussy.

Now I understood what Oscar had meant about giving me all the cock I could handle. I wanted to complain to the guys for not clearing this with me first, but I couldn't get mad at them, not with the way Jack was fucking me. Three more cocks were just what I needed. In gratitude, I returned to Oscar's shaft and really went to town on him. He blew his load, but I didn't have an opening available for long because Ron got up on the table and fed me his cock.

Now the gangbang was really on. I was a gangbang slut, just like in a porno movie. I wondered if I would feel shame later on. I didn't feel shame at that moment and I knew if three, ten or fifty more guys showed up, I would take them all on.

The five of them took me in just about every combination possible over the course of the next hour. Ron, Todd and Jack came in my mouth twice, and Oscar and

Hank managed one more time each. My mouth and throat were coated with the semen of five men, the tastes mixed together like some kind of nasty cocktail, and I felt my stomach filling up with their splooge. I thought about those urban legends of cheerleaders sucking off whole football or basketball teams and having to get their stomachs pumped because of too much semen. Maybe this was no myth after all?

But I could handle it. I could swallow more baby batter if it shot my way.

The interns were ready for more, but by then I was pretty worn out and begged off. Any protests were quickly squashed by Hank. Not wanting to anger their supervisor, the three younger guys thanked me for a great time and headed back to the picnic. Oscar and Hank were gentlemanly enough to stay with me until I got back some of my wind.

I knew I was a mess, covered in sperm and sweat. I knew I had some raunchy rancid sperm breath. Luckily, a part of the lake that was out of view of the picnickers was nearby. A quick dip in the water washed off all the obvious evidence of my gangbang. Even so, I was walking gingerly thanks to the pounding the guys had given me. It was Oscar who came up with the idea of saying I had strained something playing volleyball. Hank offered me some gum he had.

'Gum to hide the come,' he joked.

13

We all laughed.

We returned to the picnic, from different directions, five minutes apart. I stood around by a tree and thought about what I'd just done. I still didn't know if I felt guilty because if the chance came – if, say, the three interns found me and whisked me away into the bushes – I would let them, and I would love it. The only thing I was concerned about now was what my husband would say about my prolonged absence.

It turned out I had nothing to fear since he was so drunk he hadn't the vaguest idea of how long I had been gone or if I was even there. I sat next to him, informing him that I was sincerely glad he was having a good time, since I was having one as well.

We stayed at the picnic another hour before heading back home, Steve thoroughly drunk. I helped my husband to bed, no longer irritated with him since my itch had been scratched quite well and good.

Moondance
Rose de Fer

Fallen leaves crunched beneath Natalie's feet as she jumped down from the stile. A neglected path led her to a small copse of trees with an informational sign about the Six Maidens. A handful of damp and out-of-focus postcards were on offer for 50p each, along with a badly drawn map of the site. An honesty box stood impaled on a post nearby but Natalie brushed past it, ignoring its request of a pound for entrance. Such places should belong to everyone. Even though the stone circle was on private grounds, she wasn't visiting the grounds. Just the stones.

She'd only been here once before, but she remembered the way easily enough. The path wound its way up the hill, through tangles of brambles and nettles, until it opened on to a clearing at the top. She felt like a jungle explorer picking her way through the undergrowth. All she needed was a machete to slice away the thorny branches that tore at her clothes. Half an hour later she crested the rise and saw the lichen-encrusted stone circle ahead.

It wasn't a well-known or popular site and it was certainly nowhere near as awe-inspiring as Stonehenge or Avebury. It was tucked away on a muddy hill that was difficult to find and even more difficult to get to. But its obscurity and isolation were part of the appeal for Natalie. The site rewarded those who made the journey with a spectacular view. The valley spread out before her, showing off the ravishing colour palette of October. The sun was just beginning to set. Natalie shrugged off her rucksack and began to unpack beside the large recumbent stone at the centre of the circle.

As with most megalithic sites, no one knew the purpose of the Six Maidens. The informational sign hinted at ancient sacrificial rites performed on the altar stone, but Natalie supposed that was mainly to sex it up for any tourists who ventured far enough afield to visit the site. The six upright stones faced inward, leaning towards the altar as though drawn to whatever magic had taken place there hundreds of years ago. Natalie unfolded a red blanket and spread it over the altar. Then she carefully laid out her things one by one. Candles, goblets, wine.

By the time she had finished the full moon was on the rise, glowing like burnished copper in the sky. The light transformed the stones, painting them with fantastic colours as though clothing them in gowns of fire. It was a perfect night for the ritual.

Natalie poured some Cabernet into a goblet and arranged the candles along the rim of the altar. They quivered in the slight breeze, throwing eerie shadows against the stones. Leaves had gathered at the feet of the weathered Maidens like scarlet snowdrifts and small animals scurried through them, unable to conceal their presence.

Natalie took a sip of wine and began to unbutton her dress. She wore nothing underneath. The night was chilly against her bare skin but she would be warm soon enough. She kicked off her shoes and stepped forwards, gingerly placing her bare feet on the ground. Mud squished beneath the covering of leaves as she began to dance. There was no music but the sounds of the night – the crunch of dry leaves beneath her feet and the whispering of trees in the breeze. The moon hung low in the sky like a giant eye, watching her.

She made shapes against the standing stones with her body, undulating her arms, arching her back, moving sinuously through the leaves. As a child she'd had a handful of ballet lessons, but any knowledge she'd gained had long since worn off. She simply followed her body, going where it wanted, moving as it dictated. It was like being guided by an external force, as though she were at the mercy of a powerful but benign puppet master.

Natalie had always imagined that the sensation of being naked outdoors would be scary. Instead, she found it liberating. Exhilarating. Even though there was no one to see her she felt watched by a thousand eyes. The crisp air against her naked skin, the cool mud between her toes ... all of it made her feel primal and wildly sexual.

She didn't really believe all that stuff Rhiannon had told her, that dancing naked under the full moon in an ancient site would show her the face of her true love.

'Oh please,' she'd scoffed. 'I'm not after true love. Frankly, I'll settle for a good shag!'

But in the end it had seemed such a lovely and slightly transgressive idea. How could she resist? Rhiannon had taken her along to coven meetings, read her Tarot cards and given her amulets and totems over the years. And while Natalie never really felt the presence of anything otherworldly, the pagan mindset appealed to her. She liked the idea of a religion that celebrated nature and sexuality instead of focusing on guilt, shame and fear.

Her movements grew more assured and sensual. More erotic. Her hands began to move, seemingly of their own accord, to caress her breasts, her belly, her sex. Without quite realising what she was doing, she sank to her knees on the ground and let her fingers slip down between her legs, where she was very wet. Losing any trace of self-consciousness, she moaned softly as she stroked the soft folds of her labia. Images from her plentiful inventory of fantasies flashed across her mind's eye before she settled on the one she felt most fitting: the virgin sacrifice.

She pictured herself led naked into the clearing by sombre robed figures, an iron collar heavy around her neck, iron shackles weighing down her wrists and ankles. Two of the men guided her to the stone altar and laid her on her back without a word, securing her chains to rings they had bolted into the stone. The figures formed a circle around her splayed body, the flames from their torches flickering in the dark. Then, one by one, each man took his turn with her. Purifying her, defiling her. No inch of flesh was spared as they stroked her, scratched her, licked her, bit her, fucked her.

Natalie let loose a wild cry as the climax overtook her, surging through her body and then subsiding far too quickly. She blinked. She'd never come like that before. It usually took ages and she could run through any number of elaborate scenarios in her head before her body finally reached its limit. But then, it had been a long time since she'd last had sex. Proper sex, that was – the kind that left you shaken and disorientated. She collapsed in the leaves and stared up at the moon as the pulses began to subside.

'Is that it?' she asked, feeling cheated.

'Only if you want it to be.'

The deep voice made her freeze, her eyes wide and staring up into the night sky. Had she imagined it? She lay perfectly still, her ears attuned to the slightest sound. When the voice came again it was close enough to feel.

'I won't hurt you,' it said with a chuckle, 'unless you want me to.'

Instantly Natalie scrambled to her feet and covered her nakedness as a man emerged from the shadows behind the tallest Maiden.

'Who the hell are you? How dare you spy on me? I thought I was alone!'

'Obviously. But you do realise this is private property, don't you? Technically you're trespassing.'

She drew herself up defiantly. 'Fine. Call the police. Let's see what they think about a man who spies on women.'

'Who said anything about calling the police?' he asked with a good-natured laugh. 'I've as much right to be here as you. Or not, as the case may be.'

As he drew nearer Natalie's outrage faded. He was gorgeous. All he had on was a dressing gown of deep blue satin but it didn't seem at all incongruous under the circumstances. Clearly he'd had the same idea she had.

The stranger's eyes were dark and piercing and his features looked as though they'd been carved out of marble. Shoulder-length dark hair whipped around his aristocratic face and Natalie found herself wondering if the rest of him was as appealing.

As though reading her mind, he unfastened the sash

of his robe and slipped it off his shoulders to display a well-toned and muscular physique. Her eyes flicked down below his waist, but his cock was hidden in shadow. Even so, she could see he was excited. He held the robe out to her.

'It's only fair,' he said.

She took the robe and slipped it on. It was warm from his body and she tied it tightly, more to trap the musky heat against her skin than to cover herself. Then she crossed her arms with a grin as she stared brazenly at his nakedness. He raised his arms and obligingly performed a little turn for her and she drank in the sight of him.

'Mmm, very nice,' she said, noticing with pleasure that his cock was a little bigger. 'Now let's see *you* dance.'

He quirked an eyebrow at her. 'Oh, I never dance. Alone.'

She blushed as he took a step towards her, his hands outstretched as if to reassure a frightened animal that might flee at any moment. But she had no intention of running away. She stood still as he reached her and gently untied the sash of the dressing gown. It fell open, exposing her once again to the chilly night. And his hungry eyes. Natalie felt transfixed by his gaze as he slipped the gown off her shoulders and let it fall to the ground. He took her hands and led her back into the centre of the stone circle.

Natalie melted into his touch as he pressed himself

against her and she felt her sex moisten in response to his hardness. Enfolding her in his arms, he began to gently sway from side to side, the kind of slow dancing that wasn't really dancing at all. She slipped her arms around his waist, eyeing the altar stone over his shoulder. The wind lifted a corner of the blanket as though beckoning them. Natalie pressed herself against her companion, willing him to move in that direction.

But he was in control. Despite her hints he kept a firm hold on her and refused to be led. He glanced once at the altar and then back at her, shaking his head with a smile.

'Don't you want to ...?' she ventured at last in a husky voice.

He looked down into her face, his eyes gleaming in the moonlight. 'Oh yes. But don't you think we should be as nature intended?'

She blinked in confusion but before she could speak he lifted her off her feet. He held her in his arms as though she weighed nothing at all and carried her to the edge of the clearing, where the overhanging trees had shed their leaves. He deposited her in the middle of the huge pile.

Natalie lay back in the bed of leaves, delighted at the surge of unfamiliar sensations. The leaves crackled and hissed beneath her, some damp and chill, others sharp and crisp. She felt them snagging in her hair and lightly scratching her bare limbs. They smelled like the forest, pungent and piny. She knew she would forever after associate the smell with sex.

She looked up at her mysterious companion and spread her legs wide for him. The moon bathed her flesh in ethereal blue light, making her feel like a creature from another world, someone for whom the normal rules didn't apply.

'Take me,' she panted, reaching up for him.

Leaves crunched beneath him as he knelt above her. She felt the wet tip of his cock against her thigh and then he was angling her legs even further apart. She writhed, grinding her hips hungrily as he drew his fingers up along the insides of her thighs, lightly grazing her labia. His fingertips traced delicate circles over her shaved mound before moving on. He seemed determined to drive her mad with longing. He was teasing her, toying with her and clearly enjoying her lust.

Then he leaned down over her, blocking her view of the moon. His hands covered her breasts and she gasped as he slid his palms over the hard peaks of her nipples. The sensation was electrifying. She threw her arms out to each side and clutched fistfuls of leaves, tossing her head from side to side as he played with her.

At last he kissed her, but it was maddeningly tender. Aching with need, Natalie pushed up against him, urging him to bruise her with his lips. He obliged by forcing his mouth down harder on hers and plunging his tongue inside. She moaned deep in her throat, clutching his face and twining her hands in his long hair.

He pulled away and stroked her face. Natalie kissed his fingers, licking them and displaying her tongue's agility as she sucked his thumb into her mouth and ran her tongue over and around it. When he finally withdrew it she nipped gently at his palm, salivating at the taste of his hot and salty skin, eager to devour every inch of him. And be devoured in return.

He trailed his fingers down the length of her body, pausing at intervals to caress and stroke her. He returned to her breasts, pinching her nipples and brushing them gently with his lips. His warm tongue flicked over them, moistening them and making them burn when he moved away, abandoning them once more to the cold air.

His hands resumed their exploration, stroking every inch of her exposed flesh, finally slipping down to the wet crease of her vulva. She drew in a long shuddering breath as she bucked her hips beneath him, desperate to feel him inside her. Just seeing him had been foreplay enough: she'd wanted him from the very first moment. And the thought that he'd been watching her when she'd thought she was alone made her shudder with helplessness and desire.

'Please,' she moaned.

He favoured her with an indulgent smile and angled himself into position. Her entire body was trembling

24

with anticipation and she gasped as she finally felt the head of his cock demanding entry. She relaxed and he slid inside in one long exquisite thrust. With a primal cry she threw back her head, adjusting her position so he could go further, deeper. She wrapped her legs around him, hooking her feet together in the small of his back as though she could trap him there. Encircling her with his arms, he pressed his body into hers as he thrust himself in and out, filling her completely before withdrawing, only to fill her again.

Leaves rustled around Natalie's head, distorting her gasps and sighs as he fucked her. She buried her hands in his hair, smoothing it away from his face so she could see his eyes. They burned with unrestrained lust. He had abandoned his languorous pace and was taking what he wanted as much as giving her what she demanded. Natalie had always liked her sex rough and frenzied and it excited her more to see that he was losing himself as much as she already had.

Without warning her companion rolled them over until Natalie was on top. Gazing down into his eyes she felt a kind of primitive freedom she had never experienced before. She sat up, impaled on his cock, and arched her back. The moon hung above them, heavy and red.

From somewhere in the woods an owl gave a high twittering call and some other, wilder, creature shrieked as if in response. The voices of the night. Natalie could imagine they were the voices of their Celtic ancestors calling to them across time. Perhaps their pagan blood was soaked into the very leaves they were lying on now.

She clasped his hands for balance and rode him, delighted to see him losing control along with her. He closed his eyes and moaned as she swivelled her hips against him. Her toes dug into the cool mud beneath the leaves, an unexpectedly erotic sensation. A sudden impulse struck her and she clawed away the leaves on either side of them, plunging her hands into the mud and smearing it over her lover's chest. Surprise flickered in his face but then he followed suit, painting her breasts and belly with mud too.

Natalie grabbed another handful of mud and decorated his face. They might be Celtic warriors on the eve of battle, celebrating life before facing the threat of death. He followed her lead, drawing muddy fingers across the bridge of her nose and sketching spirals on her cheeks. Then he grinned and flipped her onto her back.

Laughing, Natalie flung a handful of mud at him, hitting him squarely in the chest. He pushed her down into the leaves and began to fuck her again, much harder this time. His chest pressed against hers, smearing her with more of the sweet cool mud. She adjusted herself so that each thrust made contact with her clit. She was already stimulated almost beyond endurance and she knew that would send her over the edge. In a frenzy of excitement, Natalie thrashed beneath him, digging her fingernails into his back and clawing deeply to make him hiss with pain and pleasure.

The fury of their passion forced Natalie deeper into the cushion of leaves until she could feel nothing but mud against her back. It squelched rudely as they fucked and she felt the crescendo of an orgasm. It caught her off guard, just as he had, and racked her body with spasms of ecstasy so intense it made her scream. She pressed her open mouth against his shoulder to stifle her cries as she surrendered herself to the shattering orgasm. Never before had she climaxed from sex alone and the feeling was as exquisite as it was alien.

The jolts of pleasure racked her body and she heard her companion gasp each time her sex contracted around him. Lights were still sparkling behind her eyes from her own climax when he suddenly gave a deep low groan as his body shuddered and she felt the hot jets of his seed inside her. She clung to him tightly, flexing the muscles of her sex to prolong her pleasure and enhance his.

At last they broke apart and collapsed into the leaves, limp and spent. Natalie stared at the silhouettes of the Six Maidens, all chastely averting their faces. She couldn't believe what she'd just done. And with a complete stranger! The two of them were absolutely filthy. Covered in mud and leaves. The air was ripe with the musky scent of sex and Natalie was surprised to find that she already wanted more. She reached over to caress his dozing cock. To her delight, she felt it twitch in response. She suspected it wouldn't be long before he could take her again. And again.

Then a sudden thought struck her and she sat up, glancing around nervously. 'I hope no one heard us. They'd do us for public lewdness as well as trespassing.'

'Oh, I doubt that,' her companion said with a sly grin. 'Besides, only one of us is trespassing.'

She blinked at him for several seconds before the realisation sank in. Then she blushed to the roots of her hair. 'Oh my God,' she moaned. 'Private property. Of course. I had no idea.'

He regarded her with mock seriousness. 'Well, perhaps I could be persuaded not to involve the authorities.'

Giggling, Natalie clambered to her knees and clasped her hands. 'Oh please, sir, I'll do *anything* to avoid going to jail!'

'Anything? That does rather put you at my mercy, doesn't it?'

'I can't think of anywhere I'd rather be.'

He smiled again, sexy and sinister. 'I warn you – I can be a very demanding master.'

He stood up and Natalie felt her insides flutter with desire again at the sight of him. He gently pulled her to her feet and led her towards the altar stone. The candles had burned down to almost nothing, but the moon was still gloriously bright. It illuminated the blanket, making it look as though the altar was drenched in sacrificial blood.

'Two goblets,' he said. 'How very thoughtful.'

He held them both out expectantly and Natalie obeyed the unspoken command, pouring a measure of wine into each one. They drank deeply and then he set both goblets down on the altar. Natalie trembled in anticipation. He took her by the arms and turned her around to face the stone. Then he gently pushed her down over it.

She closed her eyes as she stretched out along the length of the altar, grasping the edge of the red blanket and parting her legs to make herself an easier target. Soon she felt his cock pressing against her soft wetness and she whimpered as he entered her again. She was sore from their earlier exertions but that only seemed to enhance the pleasure.

This time he wasn't gentle. Now that he knew what she wanted, he didn't waste time with foreplay. He plunged himself in to the hilt, gripping her pelvic bones like handles as he pounded her ruthlessly. Natalie clung to the far edge of the altar under the gorgeous onslaught. The blanket did little to protect her mud-spattered breasts from the rough surface of the stone and the friction against her nipples quickly became a sweet torment. Once more her cries pierced the calm of the night as they discarded all propriety and gave themselves over to animalistic passion. She didn't even know the man's name or she would have screamed it into the trees.

Just as it hadn't taken him long to recover, it didn't take him long to come once more. And as he did he snaked his fingers around to her clit and teased it to madness again. She was hovering on the verge of another climax when she happened to glance up at the path that led into the clearing.

A group of night-time ramblers stood there, staring in open-mouthed horror at the sight of two muddy figures enacting what could only be some bizarre sexual ritual on the altar of the Six Maidens.

The soft laughter in her ear told her he'd seen them too. But he didn't stop what he was doing. He pinched her clit between his fingers and Natalie arched her body upwards, sending a cry up into the heavens as she came. Some unseen creature answered her call and then the only sound was the crunch of dry leaves beneath the rapidly retreating boots of the hikers.

Her legs were incapable of holding her up and she wilted over the stone, where she lay spent and exhausted until she felt the chill of a goblet at her lips. She lifted her head and drank gratefully, then smiled up at her companion.

'I'm Natalie, by the way.'

'Pleased to meet you,' he said. 'My name's Lucian.'

He helped her up and wrapped the blue robe around

her shoulders. He blew out the candles one by one and collected her things, putting them in her rucksack while she watched. Then he crouched down and slipped her muddy feet back into her shoes.

She offered him a rueful smile as she recalled her words earlier that night. 'So – is that it?'

He shook his head and flashed his wicked grin again. 'Absolutely not. I'm taking you back to the house with me. I've got a shower big enough for two. And a very comfortable bed.'

Natalie slipped her arms around his waist and snuggled up close to him. 'Yes, Master,' she purred.

He shook his head as though he couldn't believe his luck. 'You know,' he said, 'I never used to believe in magic. But my mate Rhiannon was right. These pagan rituals really do work.'

The Only Man Worthy
Aishling Morgan

Amelie put her finger to her lips.

'Hush, darling.'

Tom looked close to tears as he continued to beg.

'Please, Amelie. You're so beautiful, and I need you so badly. Please!'

'No, Tom, not until our wedding night. You know how I feel about that. You'll just have to do it in your hand.'

Tom's response was a hollow groan, but he flopped down into a chair and took hold of the straining erection that protruded from his open fly. Amelie watched as he began to masturbate, unable to prevent herself from enjoying her power even though it made her feel wicked. Yet there was no choice. Tom was a nice man, a kind man, also a good provider. He would make the ideal husband: faithful, gentle and patient, while his skill as an accountant ensured that she and her children would never be in want. Yet they would not be his children. That was unthinkable. The man who fathered her children would be a truly great man, a genius, nothing less.

Again Tom began to beg.

'Please, Amelie, at least take me in your mouth? Or your hand even, anything! Please, Amelie. I love you. I need your touch.'

Amelie shook her head.

'You know you shouldn't ask that of me, darling. My body is a temple, sacred until God has made us one. But I do understand your needs, so you can look, as long as you promise not to touch.'

Tom responded with an urgent nod and Amelie moved her position on the bed to allow herself to pull up the loose white dress which was all that she wore on top, showing off first her panties and then her naked breasts.

'There we are, darling. Now do be quick.'

He gave a low sob and began to tug harder on his erection. His eyes were fixed on her body, his mouth slightly open, an expression so urgent and so adoring but also so foolish that she had to suppress a giggle. Yet there was no denying that he was turning her on, but not enough to make her give up what he wanted so badly. She stretched on the bed, languid and cool as he hammered at his cock, stroking her nipples to make them stiff.

'There, darling. Does that look nice? Am I pretty?'

Tom's answer came in words gasped out to the rhythm of his now desperate masturbation.

'Beautiful. Perfect. So sweet. Oh God, Amelie ... Amelie, take your panties down Amelie ... please ... show me your bottom ... your pretty bare bottom and your lovely little cunt, please!?'

'There's no need to be dirty, Tom.'

Amelie had wagged a finger at him as she spoke, but she complied with his request, enjoying her power over him too much to want to refuse, despite his crude words. Rolling onto her knees, she lifted her bottom and reached back, to take hold of her panties and peel them slowly down. Tom gave a long, heartfelt sigh, his eyes riveted to her as she exposed herself inch by inch, the gentle valley between her firm little bottom cheeks, the tight pink dimple of her anus, and finally her virgin sex, with the red bulge of her hymen plainly visible where it held her inviolate to his cock.

'Oh, Amelie!'

He came, so copiously that he soiled not only his trousers and shirt but his own face. Amelie gave a little tut as she pulled her knickers back up, then quickly rolled her legs off the bed, speaking to him as she made for the bathroom.

'Really, Tom. I know you're a man, and men have their needs, but you really must try and show a little more restraint. I'm not a sex doll.'

He didn't answer, his eyes now closed in guilty bliss, while his mouth was slack and wider than before. Amelie knew from long experience that he would spend the next few minutes feeling bad about demanding that she surrender herself to him, and for what he'd asked of her. He'd always been like that, desperately eager to please her and pathetically grateful for what she chose to give. She liked it that way, and took care to conceal her own emotions, such as the urgent need to spread her thighs and have her soaking cunt filled with hard, eager cock.

She locked the bathroom door, as she always did, turned on the shower, slipped out of her dress and tugged her panties down a little. It had felt good with the material taut around her thighs and she wanted to feel the sensation again as she sat her bare bottom down on the toilet seat and spread her legs. Her hand went to her cunt to tease the moist flesh between her lips, and then lower to touch her anus in a moment of pure, dirty indulgence. The little hole felt tight and soft, deliciously sensitive, and for a moment she wondered if she had time to ease a finger in, only to decide to postpone the naughty pleasure for a more convenient moment. Tom was outside, waiting his turn in the bathroom, and while she knew he wouldn't make a nuisance of himself she didn't want to take too long and risk arousing his suspicions. Reluctantly, she abandoned her exploration of her bottom-hole and began to masturbate in earnest, with the ball of her thumb circling her clit and one finger gently pressed to her hymen.

Her rubbing quickly grew urgent as she remembered how it had felt to kneel on the bed with her dress pulled high to show off her breasts and her panties at half mast, the white cotton stretched taut between her thighs as she showed Tom her virgin cunt hole. It had been so good, both to be showing off and knowing exactly how he'd respond, tugging furiously at his cock in impotent desire until he came all over himself. She nearly came herself at the memory of the thick white semen erupting from his cock, but held off at the last second and turned her mind to how any real man would have behaved in the same situation.

She'd have been fucked. There would have been no begging, no pathetic entreaties. He'd have climbed on the bed behind her, given her bottom a few firm smacks to teach her not to be a tease, and pushed his cock to her cunt, to burst her hymen and fuck her until he'd added the white of his semen to the red of her deflowered sex. Maybe he'd have taken a little longer with her and made her suck his beautiful big cock for a while as he explored her body, or spanked her properly, leaving her red-bottomed and whimpering. One way or another he'd have come inside her and left her pregnant with his child.

Amelie bit her lip to stop herself crying out as she came, holding the image of her virgin cunt speared on a truly massive cock, her hole straining taut on the thick shaft, which would be streaked red and white with her blood and his semen. The only question was: who was worthy?

* * *

It was not an easy question to answer. All her life she'd been the most methodical of girls, with her progress neatly mapped out, stage by stage. So far she had successfully resisted all the boys and men who'd found her slender young body appealing, never giving in to more than the occasional blow job when one of them proved especially desirable or particularly pushy. She had done well in her exams and secured the place at university she needed to give her polish and make it easier to select a man who would make a suitable husband. That man had been Tom, who possessed all the right attributes, principally earning power and a mild, obedient nature, but he was blatantly unsuitable to be the father of her children.

So were all the other men she'd met, even the vice chancellor of the university, who'd propositioned her one evening and got his face slapped for his troubles. A mere vice chancellor was not enough. What she needed was a man whose intellect and achievements would ring down the centuries, a man whose name could claim equity with Beethoven or Churchill, with Darwin or Joyce, a true great. Unfortunately such men were impossible to identify until they had achieved their status and hard to find and seduce even then. Besides that, her timing needed to be immaculate, as in order to conceive she would have to have sex almost immediately before her wedding night and somehow conceal from Tom the fact that she had already surrendered her supposedly sacred virginity.

Yet she was nothing if not determined. Her choice was made and her plans laid. To celebrate the final days of freedom she would choose a weekend of riding in La Mancha, sat astride the magnificent Spanish palominos, which would allow for a tear-stained explanation of how she had come to ruin her hymen while providing the perfect excuse to visit a rather different destination, the villa of Vicente da Silva near Valdepenas.

Da Silva was perfect, a brilliant, fiery writer during his early years in Cuba and Central America, a man who'd fought time and again for what he believed in. He was also a composer, an athlete and, if rumour was to be believed, a dedicated lothario. Now in his seventies, he had spent the past two decades living the life of a recluse, alone in a great, decaying mansion surrounded by vineyards and olive groves, at least if the information she'd gleaned from the internet was accurate.

Amelie had no doubts at all of her ability to seduce him. A man was a man, and she had taught herself well, always ready to take in what would arouse a male, to the point at which she'd made more than one frustrated

through his shorts and massaging him gently, making her intentions even more obvious than before. He took a moment to respond and then his hand came out and made tentative contact with her back. She didn't resist, and his hand slipped lower, first to her hip and then to the turn of her bottom.

Amelie smiled in response, pushing herself out to make both her cheeks and the slit between them available to his hand. He continued to stroke and to squeeze, gradually gaining confidence as she kneaded his cock through his shorts. He reached down with his spare hand to unzip himself. Amelie took the hint and opened the button of the tattered garment to pull out a dark cock, every bit as thick and long as she'd hoped and imagined. His caresses immediately grew more urgent, eager fingers slipping beneath her bottom to find her sex.

She sighed as he touched her cunt, and pushed out her bottom a little further to invite yet more intimate exploration. He turned a little to touch her breasts, his fingers moving over the sensitive flesh as if in astonishment at the firmness of her flesh and the stiffness of her nipples. Amelie leant forwards, making her position yet more provocative and vulnerable, her bottom pushed well out behind, breasts lolling forwards. She had begun to masturbate him, rolling his thick brown foreskin back and forth across the plump pink cockhead and using her fingers to tease the most sensitive areas of his skin. Despite

41

his age, his cock had already begun to swell, growing and stiffening in her hand. He was well endowed too, with little evidence of the years, making it easy for her to take his penis in her mouth.

He tasted of salt and of man, making her more eager still. She took him deep and began to suck. He gave himself free rein with her body, his long lean fingers exploring the shape of her breasts and the stiff little points of her nipples, the curve of her bottom cheeks and the lips of her cunt and her hole. A sudden sharp pang of nervous excitement hit her as he tried to penetrate her, only to find his way blocked by her hymen. He withdrew, but only for an instant, until she'd parted her knees and pushed her bottom out into a more vulnerable position, making it very obvious she was his for the taking.

His caresses became more intimate still, his fingers rubbing in the wet slit of her cunt and probing at her hymen, his cock now a hard bar of flesh in her mouth. The discovery she was a virgin had excited him, which was exactly as it should be, and Amelie gave an encouraging wiggle as she took him as deep into her throat as he would go. He gasped in response, and for one awful moment she thought he was going to waste himself down her throat so pulled quickly back.

She didn't bother to speak, knowing he wouldn't understand and that the language of her body was all he needed. She got up to straddle him as he slipped forward a little in his chair. He took hold of his cock, holding it up to make a spear for her to sit on, his eyes fixed in wonder and delight on her naked body as she lowered herself gently onto his erection. It was the moment she'd been looking forward to for so long, when she would give up her virginity to the man she'd chosen as worthy. Despite the dull ache as the head of his cock pushed against her hymen she was in a state of ecstasy, as much spiritual as physical, as she slowly allowed her weight to settle.

He was patient, letting her take her time, only to suddenly push hard, bursting Amelie's hymen with one thrust and making her cry out at the sudden sharp pain, but also in sheer joy. Her cunt still stung as she lowered herself properly onto his cock shaft, but she was determined to cope for the sake of having her hole full, not only of erect penis, but of the spunk he had to give her. Again he began to thrust and she responded by wriggling herself down onto his cock, then lifting her hands to play with the dark mass of her hair as she rode him, showing herself off as they fucked. He gave an encouraging grin, reaching out to take hold of her breasts and pull at her nipples as his cock moved inside her, and yet he showed none of the desperation she was used to from Tom and from other lovers.

Amelie told herself that he'd probably had a thousand lovers in the course of his long and eventful life and had no doubt learnt to pace himself. In any case a man in his seventies could hardly be expected to behave like a twenty-year-old. Yet it was essential that he stayed focused on her cunt and came inside her instead of in her mouth, over her face and breasts, or any of the other dirty things men so enjoyed doing.

Eager to get him more excited, she lifted herself off his cock to turn around, exhibiting her bottom to him as he once more eased his erection up her hole. He made no comment but immediately took hold of her bottom, spreading her cheeks to show off her anus and the junction between cock and cunt as they fucked. Amelie knew she was bloody, and that he could see every rude detail as she rode him, in a way that no man had ever done before. It was gloriously dirty, almost too dirty, and she had to remind herself who she was giving such intimate pleasures to in order to let herself carry on. Yet still he showed no signs of wanting to come.

Exasperated, Amelie dismounted once more and spread herself out on the dry grass beside the chair, her thighs wide to invite entry to her freshly deflowered sex. He responded without hesitation, mounting her and driving his erection deep up her cunt even as he settled between her thighs. Amelie spread her legs as wide as they would go and took hold around his back, clinging tight as he began to hump her with an earnest enthusiasm that made her sure she'd soon be given a filling of hot sticky spunk. Only it didn't happen.

He'd been pumping away on top of her for a good

five minutes when he suddenly withdrew to kneel back and make a circular motion with one finger. The implication was obvious and again Amelie had to remind herself who he was and why it was important that she did as she was told. She got into the most vulnerable and undignified position a woman can possibly adopt, on all fours with her knees braced well apart and her bottom stuck up to expose her cunt for entry and make a blatant show of her anus.

Looking back between her dangling breasts, Amelie found his face full of lewd delight as he pulled at his cock over the sight of her spread bottom and now gaping cunt. At first she thought he was going to pull himself off and was about to speak, but he came forwards and pressed his cock to her hole filling her with thick, meaty erection. His hands took her hips and he began fucking her once more, hard and deep, and with the same even, lazy rhythm he'd used all along.

Amelie could only hold her lewd pose, her knees wide and her back pulled well in to show off her bottom to the best possible advantage as he enjoyed her cunt. He obviously appreciated the view, not only pumping in her cunt but squeezing and spreading her cheeks to enjoy the feel of her flesh and the display of her anus. Then he'd begun to spank her, chuckling to himself as he slapped at her bottom cheeks, all the while sliding his cock slowly in and out of her hole.

Only one option remained. Amelie reached back, first to squeeze his balls, then to slide a finger into the crease of his bottom to find his anus. He gave a little gasp of surprise as he was penetrated, but as she began to rub at the inside of his rectum he was gasping and immediately began to thrust deep and hard into her cunt. She pushed her finger deeper still, disgusted with herself for what she was doing but unable to deny the dirty thrill of deliberately bringing him off up her cunt hole by fingering his anus. It was working too. His hands went back on her hips and he thrust himself into her, harder and harder, until at last he jammed himself in to the very hilt and gave out a cry of ecstasy as he filled her cunt with come.

Amelie found herself smiling as she pulled her finger free. She'd done it, sweaty, exhausted, sore, but triumphant, with the great man's spunk dribbling slowly from her well-fucked hole. But one thing remained, to make very sure her womb got a good share of his seed. Even as he pulled out she was rolling over onto her back once more, to spread herself out in front of him, thighs cocked wide as she began to masturbate.

It was easy. The dirty, undignified fucking she'd been given was more than enough to spark her needs. But better still, the man whose cock she'd sucked, who she'd ridden back and front, who she'd accepted between her legs and knelt down for rear entry, who'd spanked her bottom and had her finger in his hole, was Vicente da Silva.

* * *

He watched as the beautiful, naked girl walked into his kitchen and poured out two glasses of red wine. She'd come from nowhere, a lovely young virgin, stripped, wanked him hard, sucked his cock and allowed him to fuck her in four different positions, finishing off by sticking a finger up his bottom to make him spunk inside her, and to cap it all she'd masturbated in front of him. It had to be a joke, one of his mates having a laugh by sending him a tart. Either that or she was some demented sex addict. Not that he really cared, because it had been the best fuck of his life, and no man in his right mind would have turned her down, let alone Paul Suggs, retired plumber from Penge.

Something Between Them
Ashley Hind

Hot weather makes me horny as hell. There is a simple equation I can apply: no sex for three months plus ninety degree heat equals one frustrated girl lacking her usual sense of moral decency. I had to add to this a day spent miles from home on a business course alongside mainly young males, all of whom seemed less keen on working than on eyeing me up. Their unsubtle innuendo should have made me baulk but it didn't. My usual circumspection was in constant danger of flying out the window. Although I did succeed in knocking back several hollow offers to meet up for a drink (and presumably more) that same evening, I kicked myself each time for my reticence. By the end of the day my frustrated, treacherous pussy was all but marching around carrying a placard bearing the words: *Don't listen to her – slip that big cock into me right now!*

Heat must blur the boundaries of etiquette because I was being leered at like I was a hired stripper. True, I had dressed less formally than most. A suit would have been more appropriate than my thin cotton summer dress, but I needed to take bold measures to avoid evaporating in the heat. There is something about sweat that makes me feel dirty – not in the unclean sense but in the rude sense. I guess it is by association with rampant sex. The trouble is if I sweat even a little I think it makes others believe that I'm some kind of fuck-pig that needs an instant seeing-to, like I've ceded my virtue and am available to anyone. This might not be far from the truth but I do like to cling to some vestiges of decorum. It's hard to be demure when you are leaking pints. I think that if boys see my sweat they will know I am secretly gagging for it!

I managed to get through work without having to yield my honour, although one long afternoon daydream saw me taken by all-comers in a smouldering, slithering tangle on the seminar-room floor. The day was so hot that by the end of it I felt like my insides had melted and were slowly seeping out of me and into my knickers – a dangerous thing when they are as brief as mine. Donning G-strings under a dress that only reaches mid-thigh is a bit like playing arse roulette, but unlike many girls I just love the feel of them. I love the tightness and intrusion in your rude bits. I adore the tiny slip of fabric that you don't get with fuller panties. It's just a little strip that barely covers your modesty, especially when your lips are as full as mine. If you pull them camel-toe close they cling to your shape, exposing the wrinkled-skin hint of your hair-free outer labia where they merge with your groin. You know that no matter how tight they are against you it would still only take the merest movement, just millimetres either side, to expose your slit completely. And since I have slender legs there is no flesh to hide any indiscretion. One unexpected gust could reveal everything.

Rush hour meant that the platform was packed, which also meant that getting a seat would be nigh-on impossible. I was beyond weary now. I almost screamed with the frustration of having to suffer another two hours of standing up with my pussy and my legs aching and these damn shoes killing me. The only saving grace was the slightly cooler breeze that channelled down the platform to help dry my clammy skin. However, it would be a brief respite with the train likely to be a sweat-box. The air-con would be no match for the body heat generated by the sardine tin crush of commuters. Thankfully it was on time, but as it glided in it became obvious that it was already near full, the passengers getting on at Waterloo already bagging the seats. Once it left here it would go for nearly an hour without stopping, which meant no one was getting off to create any space. It was a heart-sinking inevitability that it would be a nightmare journey.

I didn't even bother looking for a seat. I just stepped on and lodged myself into the space by the doors where I could get a decent handhold and where I was at least cut off from those lucky seated passengers by the solid partition separating the exit vestibule from the carriage. It gave me my own little square foot of space, territory that was mine, with its own small advantages to be guarded and enjoyed. There was solidity on one side giving me something nonhuman to lean against from time to time, and doors near enough to watch the world speed by and to provide an easy escape once my stop finally came. However, it wasn't all five-star luxury. I had to stand astride my bulky bag, holding it upright between my ankles, soldering myself to the spot for fear of it tipping and spreading the contents across the floor. Anything spilled would be impossible to gather up, since I was unable to bend without ramming my behind into someone's crotch. My legs were thus forced apart and I was supremely conscious of the sticky dampness between them. It seemed inevitable that the scent of my day's rudeness would seep into the air of the compartment to join the fug of the other passengers, all with a day's toil behind them. My body was covered in a sheen of sweat, my pussy felt molten, and I was surrounded by strangers.

I was thanking my lucky star that at least I wasn't too hemmed in when a group of teenage backpackers filed into the space beside me, chattering loudly in German and realising that further search would still yield no seats. They jostled around behind me, knocking me with their rucksacks before deciding that here was as good a place as any to ride out the journey time. Their loudness broke into my little corner of peace and they ate up my room, forming a wall of rucksacks to the side of me as they filled the vestibule. The rock of the train meant a backpack or two would sporadically nudge me, keeping me off balance. They were oblivious to the crush they were causing so I took comfort only from the fact that they had their backs to me and effectively sectioned me off from everything else, providing me with a cramped but secret corner of my own.

I was just coming to terms with my newly restricted space when I was jostled again from the side and looked up to see the rucksack wall being breached. First came a slender arm, soon to be followed by the rest of an annoyed-looking female. She squeezed through their ranks to force her way into my corner, right between me and the exit door. She seemed surprised and angry to find me already squashed into that precious space behind the backpackers, but the rucksack wall closed up tight again and there was no way back for her. She cursed my presence in some foreign tongue then shuffle-turned back and forth to try and find a suitable position which didn't leave her face squashed to the carriage walls or door, eventually having to grab a handle for stability. She thus ended up facing me and so close that the large bust she'd somehow contained inside her tight white T-shirt was nearly touching mine. Lucky my own tits are so much less of a handful! She smelled sweetly of a light fragrance, and I could just detect the scent of her fresh perspiration from her exertions in finding some space to stand. She was about my age, maybe mid-twenties, and Eastern European at a guess. She had dyed spiked red hair, a high, wide forehead, pale skin and bee-stung lips. She was pretty for sure, though overly made up to the point of trashiness.

She had stunning large green cat's eyes, one of which was slightly in-turned so that even though her face was barely a foot from mine I couldn't quite tell if she was looking straight at me. She certainly seemed to be and her pout was more than a little unnerving. We would generally rock back and forth in tandem but occasionally the train would cross a junction or take a sharper turn and our breasts would press gently together, holding for just a fraction before parting again. It was embarrassing but she had no room to manoeuvre and I could feel weight behind me so I dared not step back. She was tight-lipped and her eyes had narrowed and seemed to be boring into me as if it was *my* fault that we had ended up so embarrassingly close. I decided that ignorance was the best policy. If I didn't look at her then we could both pretend this social impropriety was not actually happening. The trouble was my nipples knew it *was* happening and I could feel them itching inside my bra and threatening to stand up and be counted. Worse, the naughty part of my brain – the part that annoyingly always leapt to the forefront when decorum was called for – had already decided that, despite her slightly scary demeanour, this girl was pretty enough, and our little booby-squashing antics sufficiently titillating to be used as fodder for a hot, urgent wank the second I got through my front door and tugged down my damp panties.

Then she spoke. It startled me, although her voice was not loud and was nothing like the cacophony emanating from the German kids. I didn't hear what she said. It was a short phrase, possibly not even English. I looked at her blankly.

'I'm sorry?' I said.

Her eyes turned fractionally and I saw that only now was she in fact looking at me. I felt the colour rising in my cheeks but before I could say anything else a low foreign-sounding male voice spoke from just behind me, making me jump. It was just inches from my ear – so close I could feel the breath move my hair, worsening my rapidly building jitters. I almost turned to see who this rude fellow was invading my personal space but just looking around would surely have resulted in me smacking my face splat into his nose. He wasn't actually touching me, but I could sense him right there, feel his heat, maybe even detect the fibres of his clothes against the hairs standing up on my bare limbs. Her eyes flicked away that fraction to resume her previous focus and she spoke again, not quite through me but almost, like I was invisible between her and the male companion. If her words were solid, they would have brushed my cheek on their journey to him. They took turns to speak, conversing in short, edgy phrases. It wasn't quite an argument but there was tension and impatience in her voice, although he seemed to be less agitated. I tried to lean to the side, to escape the conversation that seemed to be passing back and forth through my head, but the rock of the train kept me in the firing line and bounced me gently between their two bodies.

Her eyes would flicker back and forth almost imperceptibly as she spoke, mostly aiming at him but sometimes at me, as if she were suddenly talking to or about me. It made me jump every time, charging my belly with anxiety. Their voices dropped to hushed whispers, and her eyes fixed on me for longer, like I was definitely the target of their conversation. They were hatching something between them. I closed my ankles tighter against my bag, even though there would be nowhere for them to run if they tried to snatch it.

'I don't care!' she suddenly hissed in answer to his latest murmur, the first thing she had spoken in her accented English. 'My cunt is like a furnace and I need to come right now!'

It sent a shock jangling through me. She didn't seem to mind at all that I had heard her, not even glancing my way to gauge my reaction or witness my saucer-eyes. Her words seemed preposterously loud considering their content. I flushed with the embarrassment of being privy to them. But she could have shouted and no one would have heard her above the backpackers and the noise of the train. I felt him lean into my back, maybe due to the rock of the carriage, maybe to get closer to her to regain the circumspection she had cast aside. His voice was now more hushed and chiding, and even closer to my ear. She just tutted in response and looked more exasperated.

'Why won't you ever just fuck me when I ask?' she demanded.

It seemed extraordinary that she could be so devoid of any social graces. The heat had clearly driven her to distraction and I was seemingly the last of her worries. His words remained low and measured, still incomprehensible to me, but they were delivered right next to my ear and sent a shiver down my spine. She flashed a half-smile at his answer, then bit her lip and leaned into me, again as if I didn't exist, pressing her soft bust to mine so that she could get nearer to him.

'I can't wait to suck your big cock,' she said. 'You are such a dirty bastard I bet you've already had it up some other bitch today but I just don't care. I want every inch of it in my mouth, whether or not it is still coated in some dirty slut's come. I'll suck her clean off you and squeeze your huge tight balls because no matter how many times you have come there is still always a gallon of spunk in there to shoot down my throat.'

The words were startling and incongruous but instantly stimulating. She spoke them with her lip curled, almost through her gritted white teeth, her eyes displaying something between desire and fury: passion, I suppose. And somehow her accent made the dirty words sound more natural – not gratuitous but just plain sexy. She was right at the side of my face to deliver them too, as if they were said for my benefit as much as for his. If she had turned a little toward me and moved forward a mere six inches more she would have kissed me right on the lips. She was using me to support her weight and she just stayed there. Her warmth was scintillating but still alien and slightly oppressive, especially with me so conscious of my clammy skin. I wanted to lean back and away but that would have pressed me into him. Even from the fleeting contacts that the train movement caused I knew that his groin was right at my little bottom, the top of his hips just below mine because I have such long legs.

Her mouth had stayed slightly open and her glossy lower lip shone with the saliva beginning to pool behind it. I felt the same, like the butterfly anticipation of lust was freezing my muscles and could make me dribble at any time. I needed to close my mouth but my breath was coming too heavy now in the heat. Suddenly it felt like we were in a greenhouse, just the three of us, cut off and confined inside the stifling space. My body gave up and began to leach the perspiration so needed in its attempts to keep cool. I could feel the small drips under my armpits descend on their slow-trail journey down my sides. My bra was damp from absorbing the tiny rivulets running from my chest down into my cleavage. When he spoke I almost fainted, the jolt was so great. His voice was low but the breath went right across my ear, sending a tingling shiver rushing through me.

'If you are such a hot bitch then take your tits out,' he said. 'I want to watch you spit on your fingers and rub the wetness into your fat nipples. I want you to pinch and stretch them for me. You know I love to see your tits covered in spit and pussy juice.'

It was only the last part that made me realise it wasn't me he was talking to. I felt her exhale on my cheek and lean further into me. My own nipples immediately swelled up, their covering bra fabric too thin to possibly mask the growth. I knew she would feel them pressing into the softness of her chest, just as I now felt hers on mine. I had never so much as kissed a girl, yet here I was with some scrumptious, anonymous minx rubbing her engorged teats against mine. She smiled broadly at his suggestion, closing her eyes for a second or two, perhaps debating whether or not to do as he said and pull her top off to let her big soft tits bounce free. My mind was full of her doing his bidding and then offering her spit-wet, swollen nipples up to my waiting mouth. The jagged-cut hair by her ear was dark with dampness and I knew she would register the cool bursts of my faltering breath upon it. It was just as well she was oblivious to my presence because I was falling apart and losing the battle to disguise my excitement. She slowly opened her eyes again and said:

'I want you to beat my bare ass with your stiff prick and give me the spanking I need. You should feel how hot and sweaty my ass-crack is right now. You should wipe the head of your cock between my fat cheeks, right down over my wet, dirty holes, and then make me suck you clean.'

I could feel the heat between my own buttocks, the tightness of my knicker-string between them soaking up the pungency. My bum is only small but heat like this takes no prisoners. I shivered again at the thought of my underwear being peeled off my cunt and pulled down, of a cock – *his* cock – sliding in the warm moistness between the cheeks of my bent-over arse. I couldn't fight the words now. My shock was rapidly being overrun by lust and every word uttered would go straight to my sex, whether I liked it or not. At some point during her filthy sentence I had closed my eyes and they had remained shut. Everything else but their rudeness would now be blocked out. I was praying that it would continue and it did, her dirty goading spurring him into a response.

'As soon as I get you alone,' he said, 'I'm going to bend you over and slam my cock all the way up your slushy cunt. I want to feel your juice squelching out onto my balls. I'm going to hold your arms behind your back and push your face into the pillow and fuck you so hard you'll think my prick will come out of your mouth.'

Despite his coarseness he spoke softly, just fractions from my ear. Even though she was pressed against me with her cheek almost alongside mine, everything he said seemed like it was just for me. My puss was indeed slushy. The thin gusset of my knickers was bravely clinging on for dear life but it was already sodden and fighting a losing battle to hold back the deluge which would surely soon escape and trickle down my open thighs. My head had been muzzy from the heat but the adrenaline surge had cleared it and his words were converted into instant imagery. I already had a picture of him in my mind: dark, haughty and unshaven; his naked torso glistening with the film of sweat upon it; his hair dripping from the swelter; one hand gripping his thick bare cock and guiding it to my proffered backside, ready to drive it into my defenceless, slippery puss. It was so odd to have this person so close, speaking so intimately right into my ear, and yet to not even know what he looked like, except in my head.

'Once my prick is deep inside you I will make you come by sliding my thumb all the way up your damp, smelly ass.'

She gasped and I nearly did too, but I managed to bite my lip and hold it in, bizarrely worried that if they heard a peep from me it would alert them to my presence and break the spell. As if they couldn't see or feel me! He knew for sure that I was there because his lips had turned in closer and were now nearly brushing my ear. I could feel the soft puff of his exhalation on the tiny hairs on my lobe. I was waiting for his tongue-tip to snake out and trace an electric path across my sensitive skin, but it never came. Just as well. If it had I would have shrieked and leapt a mile, or dissolved into a climaxing heap. He must have felt me trembling but he showed no mercy and just kept up with his dirty talk.

'When you have saturated my cock I am going to take it out and slide it all the way up your sweaty, dirty arse. I'm going to make you take it all, even if you have to hold your butt cheeks apart to let me in. I want to feel my balls on your cummy snatch. I might even push them inside so you can cream all over them too.'

Her breath was coming in pants and her chest was heaving, her nipples riding up and down over my own. Her heat was too much and I knew the sweat would be seeping from my chest and soaking my dress. Once she pulled away I would be left with a circle of dampness on my front for all to see, and everyone would know that I was a dirty bitch on heat. She was no better. She had moved her hips forward and I could feel her short skirt riding up against my thigh. Her legs were also bare and smooth, but hot too, so that when we were rocked into contact our skin seemed to fuse in our moisture, sticking tight and clinging jealously so that you could actually hear the sound as the train motion peeled us apart. Every time we joined again we were more clammy and adhesive than before, and each time we were this close I swear I could smell the sweet muskiness of her desire creeping up between us. I thought that at any time she would grab me, grip my arse and hold me tight to her, riding my thigh like a wanton tart until she came.

'Give me your cock,' she said, her voice cracking with urgency.

He ignored her, leaning into me with the rock of the train but staying there, allowing a tentative contact against my back and pushing his hips forward a little, so that I could just sense a hint of his stiff, constrained prick at my bottom. Then the train jolted and there was no mistaking his erection bulging beneath his clothes and pressing into my arse, trying to bury itself along my damp crack. I should have jerked away but I didn't. I could feel the pulse of his cock even through the combined layers of our clothing. It ran the whole length of my bum and felt like an iron bar. I could hear his breath coming quicker too now. I was sure he would put his arms around me and draw me in but he did not. I stayed bolt upright, desperate for their bodies to close in and sandwich me, my head full of visions of this huge prick inside my tight passage, absolutely ready to spurt, and of the endless torrents he would bless me with. He must have read my mind.

'I'm going to make you suck my cock straight out of your ass, right to the hilt. I want to watch you cram all your fingers inside your mushy cunt while you suck me and take all my spunk to your face.'

The desire was more evident in his speech now, the whisper becoming more of a hiss as he forced the filthy words out, and I felt a droplet of spittle hit my cheek as he said the word *spunk*. If he was starting to lose control, hers had all but evaporated. I expected her hands to be all over me, to be grasping and squeezing my tits and arse. I expected her to be thrusting her tongue down my throat. She did none of these things. She stayed as she was, pressing against me, radiating her heat into me but otherwise ignoring me completely. I was desperate to kiss her but I could not. Everything so far was intimate and illicit but at least it was unseen; a kiss would be overt and obvious and would ruin it all. If I stayed quiet and kept my head then no-one else would spot our little oasis of dirtiness within the baking desert of tired, glum, sweating commuters. I could feel the moisture from her mouth like a miniature cloud against my face with each heavy breath forced out of her. I knew her pussy would be raging just like mine, but while I had to stay silent, she could give vent to her lust.

'Give me your cock,' she said again, but this time it was an order. 'I need your cock right now. Give it to me!'

I felt his hand at the small of my back, finding a way between our close bodies. His knuckles pressed my dress to my skin and I could feel the coolness of the sweat-soaked fabric. His hand inched down between us. I felt it at the top of my bum, just above my little jut. Then the back of his hand was brushing my rump and nudging it. I realised what he was doing an instant before I heard his zip come down. He exhaled hard into my ear with the relief of freeing his restrained erection. My blood was bubbling inside me and I felt the fear of anticipation but still I didn't dare open my eyes and break the spell. She was whispering *give it to me*, again and again, right into my ear. It meant her lips must have been nearly touching his. I felt his chest slide down my back a little, like he was bending his knees. As he came up again I sensed the brush of my dress against the backs of my thighs and knew instantly that my skirt was being lifted, although I could not feel his hands. Then I felt *it*. His huge bare prick was under my dress, the head resting just beneath my bum cheeks. Then it was inching forward between my parted legs, the upper side of his erection sliding inexorably along my wet gusset, the pressure of it wringing the juices from the sodden fabric to coat his skin. I could feel the gusset beginning to string, shrinking away as wetness defeated it, sure soon to be swallowed between my ready lips as they swelled to meet his bareness. The tingle of his skin on mine was jellifying and it didn't stop until his groin was pressed hard against my buttocks. Only his girder cock was holding me up at all. I was praying my saturated knickers would dissolve in my oozing lust so that I could soak the fat meat throbbing hot against me. I knew if I looked down I would have seen the tip of his great prick tenting the front of my dress, but I didn't dare open my eyes.

She knew what he had done and reached up, her hand also going under my clothes and sliding up my thigh to cup his cock and hold it to my puss. It was almost burning me. She pressed his length to my slit and I could feel the itch of my knicker material inside me. Her fingertips were lightly skimming the delicate bulges of my exposed outer lips, her nails tickling me, making my knees buckle, forcing me harder against him. *Oh God* I was thinking but she was saying it for me, over and over, in breathed whispers. She was running her fingers underneath his prick and this made her palm squash against my throbbing clit. He was very gently moving back and forth, secretly sliding his cock against my barely covered quim. The heat between us was almost overwhelming and the drops were now running freely from my temples and down the side of my face, where her lips made their light contact.

'I want to fuck you right now,' he said. 'I want to bury this pole inside you and slap it in and out of your fat, saturated cunt until you faint.'

I could feel her pressing harder, her fingertips fluttering against me as she moved her hand over his length. Then she was tickling me, a purposeful action this time and not just a by-product of her wanking motion on his cock. It was the only suggestion I got from her that I was actually a part of their sex game and not some gooseberry who had inveigled her way in and somehow found herself entwined in the masturbation of his big prick. Her nails were skimming over the puffy skin of my labia and grazing the fabric of my stretched-taut knickers. Then with one deft movement she slid her fingers across my puss and took the gusset with them. My cunt was so hot and swollen it felt like a feasted belly popping open a shirt. The gusset stayed firmly to the side, exposing my slit completely so that it spread apart warm and slippy across the top of his shaft and bathed him in another rush of escaping juices. The blissful heat of our naked flesh together almost made me pass out. She continued to press him up into me and tease my lips with her fingernails. I couldn't help but tense my arse over and over, sending my hips forward in little jerks that slid me back and forth along his length. His cock was straining against me and his breath was coming in sharp bursts, but still his dirty-talk continued.

'I want to see you sit on some skinny English bitch's face and grind your nasty hot arse into her so hard her nose goes up your shit-hole and stops her from breathing. I want to see you wipe your cunt juice all over her, just like you did to that whore you met on the bus. I want you to make her taste your ass, to stick her tongue right up inside you, and I want you to reach forward and spank her pussy if she doesn't do it right.'

I was still buttoning my lip to avoid giving myself away but I was riding his cock harder now, trying to wriggle down onto him and then jam my clit into the heel of her hand on my forward stroke. My saturated quim had spread apart with his shaft between my swollen lips. My excitement seemed to be flooding out of me, tainting the stale air with the obvious smell of sex. Still I could not stop myself. If I opened my eyes the enormity of what I was doing in that so-public place would have stopped me in my tracks. It seemed impossible that our act could not be seen, hidden only by my skirt and from the sheer closeness of those around us. Our noise was masked only by their noise, our smells only by theirs. I kept my eyes closed and kept riding, driven on by the knowledge that I was nothing but a skank being used by these dirty bastards for their filthy act, and that I need not be there at all if not to provide them cover and lubrication for his cock. Even as I was so close to coming she still did not kiss me. She had a firmer grip of his prick to make a closed seal between my body and her hand and I realised that her fingers were moving on his length too, trying to coax his spunk out. He was so close and yet not quite ready.

'I want to watch her ride your strap-on so I can get behind her and slide my prick into her ass. Then we can fuck both her holes at the same time, just like we did to that black bitch with the fat butt – the one who squirted all over you when she came. I want to take my cock out and spunk all over both your filthy cunts.'

That was it for me. I tensed my thighs to keep her hand and his prick hard against me and I thrust forward over him and into her palm. The pleasure came in such a hot rush I felt sure I would black out. I bucked against him and felt her frantically wanking him from below. I bathed his shaft and her hand, my hot torrent flowing out as they supported my buckling weight. I humped him fast as the heat pounded in my head and threatened to burst me. I finally opened my eyes and looked down. My flimsy dress was rucked up around my middle exposing me completely. His huge, bulging cock-head was sticking out between my thighs, rammed tight up into my slit. She was still cupping his shaft and pressing it up into me from below. Her other hand was clutching the gathered hem of her dress, holding it up to expose her tight white panties and the clearly-defined split of her own sex beneath. She was jerking her hips back and forth too, rubbing his straining glans hard against her covered clit. The tingling friction of the ever-so-slightly coarse fabric of her panties clearly drove him over the edge. He gasped and soaked her panties with a deluge of hot spunk. The exhilaration of seeing his pulsing pent-up prick shoot was almost enough to make me come once more.

When he began to slump she put her hand to her crotch and rubbed the sticky lumps of his come into her filthy knickers with a shiver and a sigh of pleasure. Then she let go of her dress and it fell to cover our crime. She unstuck herself from me and opened her eyes, and I watched her mouth spread into a smile of delight. Then she shuffled around to face the rucksack wall, standing as if nothing had happened, staring silently into the backs of the noisy German kids. I could already feel his hand at my bottom, working away to stuff his still-twitching prick back inside his pants. I heard the faint noise of the zip and then he too stepped back. The sudden cooling of my soaked dress spread an unwelcome shiver over my skin. My legs were still shaking and I had to lean hard against the partition to relieve some of the weight. Tiredness was sweeping over me and I knew I must look a terrible state: sweat-damp, flushed and dishevelled. I must have looked and smelt like I had just come.

My dress had been hit by a spunk-blast rebounding off her crotch and carried a noticeable, round, glue-like stain. I could smell her fragrance and his seed upon me. Every passenger in the carriage would smell our fuck and see me in my flustered state and know what I had done. If they held up my dress they would see my pointless, cum-steeped knickers rolled into a string and pulled to the side of my mound to expose my guilty, glistening puss. There was nowhere to run and nowhere to hide, so I just leant panting against the partition with my eyes closed, waiting for the whispers and the repercussions. I barely noticed the train pulling in but the door opened and the crush of bodies around me swept noisily out, and beautiful cool air breezed in to fill the vacuum, carrying its freshness into the carriage to take away the heavy smell of my dirtiness. The train pulled out and I sensed the emptiness and quiet all around me. The chatter had stopped and I could feel the relief of air all around me to ease my heavy breaths and to dry my sodden clothes and hair. I opened my eyes at last and to my utter joy I found myself all alone.

Shelf Pleasure
Justine Elyot

By the time I've crossed the disabled parking bays I'm already nagged by a sense of disappointment, convinced that he isn't here, that he's changed his routine or left town or, worse, he's avoiding me. But that's a tad dramatic, not to mention self-centred, when I've no evidence that he's even registered my existence.

I take myself to task in the trolley park for building this minor twice-weekly frisson into, well, a *thing*. It's a silly piece of self-indulgence to get me round the aisles in one piece. Magically, it deafens me to the shrieking demands of toddlers, the grumbling trolley-barging of pensioners, the general miasma of despair that hangs around the comestibles of my local BargainBuy. It isn't a thing. It's a nothing.

The trolley doesn't want to leave its rank and I rattle the handle a bit, yanking it back from the close embrace of the one behind with more force than should be necessary.

'For fuck's sake,' I say under my breath, releasing it from its trap. Preparing to direct it towards the automatic doors, I look over my shoulder, suddenly worried that some arbiter of good shopping behaviour has witnessed my outburst. It's worse than that though. *He* is standing behind me and I can't avoid meeting his eyes during the re-orientation of my face.

This has happened before, this meeting-of-eyes scenario. It goes like this: eyes meet, they drop immediately, heads turn away, then quickly turn back, eyes meet again for a fraction of a second before contact is terminated. This is the eighth time. Would a small smile of recognition be appropriate to celebrate the occasion? No, it wouldn't. He just heard me swearing, for fuck's sake. He'll be disgusted and appalled by me.

Also, he might have noted that I'm wearing lipstick and a skirt today and wonder why the hell I've dressed up to go to BargainBuy ... but no. Of course he won't have noticed that. Of course not, stupid.

I wheel away at a brisker than brisk pace and take refuge in the fruit and veg. My tactics are the same as ever. I enter the shop ahead of him and time the nego-tiation of each aisle so that I can watch him advancing towards me, stopping to pick things up, frown at labels, drop things in the trolley, flick his eyes up to the end of the row where I am 'absorbed' in checking the sell-by date of whatever happens to be the last product on the shelf.

How's he getting his five a day today? Courgette, aubergine, honeydew melon, coriander, tomatoes. Moussaka? Ratatouille? Then he picks up strawberries and I frown, picturing him dipping them in cream and feeding them to a girlfriend.

He looks up at me then, from about three feet away and holds the look.

This is new.

He's warning me. *Stop stalking me. I'll call security.* I grab my handle and flee to bread and bakery.

'Hang on.'

I look back. Is he talking to me? I think he is. I edge back towards him, liking the sound of his voice, which is exactly as I imagined it. The fact that I've imagined it suggesting that I open my legs and take it like the whore I am causes me to flush and swallow nervously, as if he can hear my fantasies.

He's holding out the punnet of strawberries.

'Do these look ripe to you?' he says.

I look up at him. He looks … sane. Sexy as ever, with an earnestness in his eyes that could be real or a ploy. I peer into the box.

'I suppose so. They aren't green or anything.'

'It's just that I can't smell them. There's usually a smell

73

with strawberries, isn't there? Kind of fruity and lush. Can you smell anything?'

The way he said *fruity and lush* definitely sounded suggestive. Or is this just a wish-fulfilment dream?

I bend and take a lungful of air.

'There's a hint of strawberry,' I say. 'But I don't think they're properly ripe, no.'

'Hmm. Shame,' he says. 'I like them really, really ripe. Bursting with juice, y'know, so it runs down your chin and you have to lick it off.'

There's not much I can do in response to that but stare, through half-closed eyes, and try not to let my tongue hang out. He has the kind of low voice and drawly northern accent that can make anything sound filthy, but even so, that had to be a come-on ... didn't it?

'I prefer cherries,' I say, trying to prolong the conversation.

'What kind of cherries?' he asks with exaggerated interest. 'The dark, intensely flavoured kind or those sticky bright red ones that look as if they've been smothered in lip gloss?'

At the mention of lip gloss, he looks at my lips. I press them together and plump them up. I'm pretty sure I run my tongue along the lower one. He'll be asking me my going rate in a moment.

'Oh, all of them,' I blether. 'Any cherries. Especially on a cocktail stick.'

He chuckles at that.

'Oh yeah,' he says. 'Cocktails.' (I'm not sure he emphasised the first syllable as much as I think he did.) 'Cocktail cherries are my favourite.' He looks down at the forgotten strawberries. 'I'll put these back then and maybe get some cherries instead.'

Fear that I am making a fool of myself consumes me once more and I simply shrug and say, 'If you want,' and run off to the safety of the croissants.

Surrounded by wholesome wholemeal, I try to review the situation. What was that all about? What did it mean? Was he flirting with me? Should I have flirted back a bit more?

'Nice baps,' says a familiar voice at my shoulder and a long hand reaches across my chest to pick up a four-pack of burger buns.

It's such a cliché of classic innuendo that I am left in no doubt. His intentions are impure. In my wicked delight I whip around and wag a finger at him, feeling like Barbara Windsor in a Carry On film. 'Ooh, cheeky!'

'I've been watching you for weeks,' he says, still standing behind me, lowering his head for better access to my ear.

'Have you?'

'C'mon, you must have noticed. I was a bit worried you'd think I was stalking you.'

'Oh!' I twist my neck. My heart pounds. 'So was I.'

'Really?'

I look down at his feet, which are big, and wonder for the millionth time whether that shoe-size-cock-size ratio thing is a myth.

'Kind of,' I mutter.

'So you were checking me out while I was checking you out?'

'Maybe.'

'Don't say 'maybe'. Look at me.'

When I do, his eyes almost glitter. He reminds me of a predator about to make his strike. My legs weaken and my clit pulses.

I take a huge lungful of fresh-baked-bread smell and lean on the shelf for support.

'I like the way your arse moves when you push a trolley,' he says in a shade above a whisper while people mooch past, oblivious. 'Especially today, in that tight skirt. When you bend down to pick up a can from the bottom shelf, it drives me wild.'

'Oh yeah?' My answering whisper wavers. You could cut the sexual tension with a knife, or maybe feed it through the bread-slicer on the counter.

'Oh yeah. Do it for me now. Bend over and pick up that bag of doughnuts down there.'

'Doughnuts? Which ones? The ring ones?'

'No, I prefer a hole to be filled. With something sweet and sticky.'

'Jam, then?'

He laughs. 'Or toffee.'

'Filthy pervert. Toffee has no place in a doughnut.'

'Sounds like I need to teach you a thing or two ... about doughnuts.'

He hasn't touched me yet, but I feel as if he's all over me somehow and I'm hot and squirmy.

'Okay.' I swallow, turn and march towards the shelf in question. I look around to make sure no stray shoppers are watching, lean down extra low, giving my bum a full-bore wiggle. I think the hem might be showing a glimpse of stocking top and suppress a giggle, picturing the effect that sight might have on him.

I pick up the doughnuts – jam – and turn to face him. He looks positively ill with lust. I think that flash of stocking top must have happened.

'I like this game,' I tell him, handing over the artery-cloggers. 'What's my next challenge?'

He opens the bag, takes out a doughnut and bites into it.

'Hey, you can't –'

He points to the bar code label and shrugs.

What he does next is infinitely more disturbing. He finds the jammy part and shoves it up to my mouth.

'Lick it,' he says. 'Go on. Lap it up.'

'I can't!'

'You can. I know you can.'

He is wicked, and he makes me want to be wicked. Tentatively at first I extend my tongue and take the tiniest dot of the sweet red filling.

'Mmm, is that nice?' he purrs. 'Get stuck in, go on.'

I push my tongue into the hole and scoop out the jam until it is all gone and my face is sticky with sugar crystals.

'Let me help you.' He puts the half-eaten doughnut back in the bag. He hustles me into an alcove between the sliced white and the speciality loaves, takes my chin in his long fingers and, oh my God, *what is this?*

He licks each grain of sugar off my skin with his warm wet tongue while I gasp and grab the pillar for support.

'There,' he says. 'Your face tastes really nice. What are your lips like?'

But I'm beyond speech. This seems to have gone wildly out of control very quickly. Should I be scared? My body seems to have replaced the fight-or-flight response with the fuck-or-fuck response.

'Do you mind if I try them?'

All I can do is shake my head.

He presses his lips to mine and they feel every bit as good, as full, as hungry as I imagined they would. *I'm getting snogged in a supermarket.* The realisation floods my knickers. I grind myself against his crotch, finding bruising hardness there. His tongue unfurls inside my mouth and his hand reaches for my hip and slides around behind, covering my arse and taking a squeeze.

The sound of ostentatious throat-clearing prevents us from going any further. A thunder-faced bakery assistant shoos us away.

'Man cannot live on bread alone anyway,' says my supermarket suitor airily. 'I think you need meat.'

I take my trolley and he stands behind me, his hands on mine, and pushes it along from my rear to the meat aisle. I wonder if the refrigerated air might dampen his ardour, but his erection crushes itself against my bottom with persistent force despite the chill.

'You're going to make some obvious joke about sausages, aren't you?' I say.

'Me? I wouldn't dream of making lewd pork product-based puns. I can't think of anything *wurst*.'

I kick his ankle. 'Enough of that. What's your name anyway?'

'Serge.'

'Serge? Are you French?'

'No, my mum just had a thing about Serge Gainsbourg. How about you? Are you named after a parental heart-throb too? Brigitte? Agnetha? Princess Leia?'

'Emma.'

'Emma Peel? That figures.'

'No, just Emma. Jeez. I'm glad we skipped the chatting up stage and just got on with business. You're quite annoying, you know.'

'I'm just nervous.'

79

'Oh, come on.'

'I am! Look at this hand – it's shaking.'

He waves his palm beneath my nose, demonstrating the fact.

'Why are you nervous?'

'Because I don't know if I can make it out of this supermarket without ripping your clothes off and taking you on the fish counter.'

'You'll get arrested.'

'I know. Hence the nerves.' The trolley comes to a halt by the bacon. 'I have to admit something too. But you'll think I'm weird. I don't think I can tell you.'

'Oh, don't tease. Confess all. I won't judge, I promise.'

'You will. You'll judge me. OK then – but don't laugh. I find supermarkets sexy.'

'What?'

'All the produce. All the ripeness and plenty, you know. Abundance and wealth. It's kind of … arousing. I often think of doing it in a supermarket.'

'That really is weird. Besides, you couldn't do it in a supermarket. It's just too busy.'

'No it isn't. Know how I know? Because I've done it.'

'You haven't!'

'I used to work here, one hideous summer after A levels. I lost my virginity in here.'

'Oh, you little liar!'

'I'm not, I swear.' He laughs. 'In about ten minutes,

they'll change shifts. These guys will all go home and a new lot will come in. There's a half-hour window after that before anyone takes a break ... which means an empty staff room ... which means ...'

'You aren't serious? You're serious!'

He snakes a hand beneath my skirt, hiding my legs behind his.

'Deadly serious. I want to feed you these cherries. Come on.'

We abandon my trolley there amid the meat and Serge takes me in one hand and his basket in the other before heading purposefully towards the double doors at the back from which the trays of fresh produce emerge all day long.

'We'll be spotted,' I moan.

'No we won't. I know this place like the back of my hand. Trust me.' He grins down at me. 'I'm a doctor.'

'*Are* you?'

'Yeah.'

'You'll get struck off.'

'Don't be silly' We are through the double doors and he swerves to the right, leading us through the middle of some shelving instead of into the centre of the room, where shelf-stackers are sorting goods and loading up pallets. At the end of the row, another door leads into a corridor. We flit past the door marked STAFF ROOM and head into the room at the end, which turns out to be staff toilets.

'We'll wait here,' he murmurs, hustling me into a stall in the Ladies'. 'Ten minutes. I promise.'

'You haven't actually asked me if I want to have sex with you in the BargainBuy staff room,' I point out.

'Don't you?' He has his hand on the back of my neck, preparing to move in for the killer kiss, but he pauses for a moment, pouting at me. 'You mean you'd leave me here with my lonely bachelor basket and go back to your trolley? What's he got that I haven't?'

I aim a gentle kick to his shin, but I'm fooling nobody. I want him so badly he must be able to smell it on me.

'A four-pack of plums.'

'Ah, if it's plums you want ...'

I give up. Doctor or not, nobody would be able to misdiagnose the shocking case of lust that has me in its grip.

Our mouths come together again and we cling to each other like spider monkeys. I am crushed up against the partition, feeding on him, when the external door opens. I stiffen and try to push him off but he holds me very still, locking me into the kiss.

'Yeah, can you believe she said that?'

The sound of bags being unzipped, lipsticks uncapped, hairspray sprayed.

Serge puts a hand on my hip and starts rucking my skirt up, slowly, gently.

'Fucking bitch. As if she never slacks off. Did you see

her yesterday, all over the bakery manager when she was supposed to be on the tills?'

The skirt is high on my thigh, Serge's fingers collecting the fabric until he holds a great fistful.

'Ugh, he's such a creep too. Silly cow. She thinks she's above the rest of us. I want to slap her one.'

Serge's other hand creeps around to my bottom, rubbing it through the satiny fabric of my knickers.

'Eh up.' The woman's voice hushes to a whisper. 'That toilet's engaged. Better watch what you say.'

He moves lower, stroking the bare part of my thighs above the stocking tops, fingers fluttering lightly around to the sensitive inner skin. I quiver and try not to pant.

'Hello,' says the second voice stridently. 'Who's there?'

I am caught in a bodily dilemma, on alert and yet unable to resist Serge's continuing campaign of seduction. The confusion bats me from one extreme to the other – tension, sex, fear, lust.

Luckily the stalls aren't the kind you can peer into.

The women continue to make gruff overtures to us, while Serge plunges his hand inside my knickers and moves cunning fingertips over my fat wet clit.

'I reckon someone's shagging in there,' says one of them suddenly. 'Come on, let's go out and see who's missing. Hey, what if it's Sheila?'

They cackle hysterically and then the door bangs shut.

Serge spears a couple of fingers inside me and pumps them back and forth with efficient rhythm. The kiss has wrecked our lips by now and he breaks it momentarily to whisper, 'You're a bad girl, aren't you, getting fingered in a lavatory.'

'You're the bad one,' I gasp. 'What if they come back?'

'They won't. It's home time. They've got bigger fish to fry. Give it five minutes and the staff room'll be safe.'

'Why the staff room? Why not here?'

'I can't get me cherries out in a public restroom. It's not hygienic!'

'Is what you're doing now hygienic then? Oh God.' His fingers speed up, pronging me with deadly accuracy while his palm slaps against my clit. I widen my stance, pushing down, urging him on until the sweet faraway tingle hits my groin and begins to spread and build, heading for the inevitable conclusion.

'I'm going to come,' I jerk out. 'I'm going to come getting fingered by a strange man in a supermarket toilet, oh yes, yes.'

I crumple against him. I've never felt so dirty, never felt so excited.

'That's a fair summing up of the situation,' he says in a low, broken croon. He kisses my defeated lips. 'And now you're going to come getting fucked by a strange man in a supermarket staff room. Let's do it.'

I freeze at first, terrified of discovery, but Serge yanks

me out and checks the coast is clear before rushing me into the empty staff room.

He pushes the water cooler up against the door and pulls down the blinds.

'Safe sex,' he says with a raffish smirk. 'Mustn't forget to take precautions. Now.'

He seats himself on a tattily upholstered green chair and plonks the basket down at his side.

'Come and eat my cherries.' He slaps the knee of one elegantly crossed leg.

I look around, as if expecting a third party to materialise from behind a dusty pot plant.

'I'm waiting.'

I take a step towards him and he reaches out, lightning quick, and pulls me onto his lap, making me straddle him with my skirt high around my waist again. His erection pushes my damp knickers up between my pussy lips. He squeezes my arse, demanding and urgent, then lifts my top over my breasts and explores inside my bra cups with his tongue and teeth.

'Cherries?' I ask from somewhere inside my fog of intense lust.

'Oh yeah. I got mixed up. Thought these were them.' He kisses a nipple then reaches down into the basket for the paper bag of dark, stone fruits.

He holds one to my lips and I bite into it. It's at that perfect point of ripeness and the juices stream down my chin. I'm going to have purple stains all over my clothes, sticky patches on my bare thighs. We share the cherries, taking a bite each, or passing them from mouth to mouth, popping the stones back into the bag when we remember what we're doing. He takes one and crushes it down inside my bra. The magenta juice seeps into the white satin cup so it looks as if my nipples are bleeding strange coloured effusions. He smashes the fruit against my nipple; it feels cold and tingly, then warm as his tongue laps it up and his teeth nip at it.

He pushes them between my sex lips, drenching them in my juices before eating or feeding them to me, letting them disintegrate in the hot clasp of my cunt so that I am cherry flavoured.

'I want to eat them out of you,' he whispers, 'but I don't think we've got time and I really need to fuck you now. Can we do that next time?'

'Yes, yes,' I say urgently, tugging at his belt. I want him inside me, a good hard replacement for the soft, squashy fruit.

He's had the presence of mind to grab a pack of condoms from the pharmacy shelves and he skins one on the moment his cock escapes from the dark fabric of his trousers. I move my knickers to one side and lower myself down on the rubbered tip, enjoying its wideness against my opening, circling my hips to tease until he grabs them, holds them still and pushes his way inside.

Oh yes, that feels full, that feels luscious. I sit back and revel in the sensation for a moment while he slips one hand back up to my breasts and flicks at the nipple.

'How's that?' he asks in a barely-there murmur.

'Amazing. You feel amazing.'

'Good. 'Cause you're going to be feeling amazing a lot from now on. You're made to be fucked, aren't you?'

'Am I?'

'Oh yeah.'

He pushes up, signalling that I should start to grind. I take him all the way in and work his shaft hard, squeezing my muscles together to milk him dry, taking it slowly so I hear him moan, quickly so I hear him pant, licking his sensitive neck until he goes wild and pinches my hips hard, holding me in position while he powers into me.

I lean into the angle I need and hold tight as my second orgasm rips through me. My head blurs, my eyes sting and when everything clears, he is making a series of grunts and throwing me around on his lap, enjoying an orgasm that seems to go on and on.

The poster on the wall behind the chair advises all staff to wash their hands before handling food. I read it before letting my head drop onto Serge's shoulder.

'We should go,' he yawns, but he doesn't sound very connected to reality yet.

I look up at the clock. That half hour's grace he mentioned is almost over.

'Come on.' I lift myself off him and try to find my feet, kissing him on the way down. 'You have to pay for that stuff.'

* * *

At the checkout, the cashier eyes us askance as she puts the stained, half-empty bag of cherries, the open doughnut wrapper and our generally shambolic shopping through the scanner. The open condom box draws a particularly fierce pursing of lips.

But when she looks up at Serge, her expression changes. 'Oh, Serge,' she trills. 'It is you, isn't it? How are you these days?'

'Hey, Maggie,' he says. 'Very well, thanks. Working up at St Faith's now.'

'Step up from here,' she replies. 'And is this your wife? Girlfriend?'

'This is my partner in crime,' he says, pinching my bum so that I startle. 'Emma.'

She looks me up and down and there's a twinkle in her eye that says *I know what he's been doing to you*. I flush and concentrate on packing the bag.

'You want to watch him in supermarkets, love,' she said. 'He was always getting into trouble when he used to work here. I suppose there isn't so much chance of that at St Faith's.'

'Most of the people I work with are out of it,' he says ruefully. 'I'm an anaesthetist. It's nice to see people with their eyes open occasionally.'

She smiles. 'Just their eyes? That'll be twenty-seven pounds fifty, love.'

Outside in the car park, there is a moment of awkwardness. I have packed all our groceries together, mine and his combined.

'How much do I owe you?'

'Oh, sod that, I'm not going through the receipt doing sums,' he says. 'Let's sort it out when we get back to my place.'

'Oh, we're going back to your place, are we?'

'Or yours. Either way. We've got some cherries left, haven't we?'

If you're ever in the BargainBuy off the main town roundabout, watch out for frottage in the fruit aisle, canoodling in the canned goods. You never know what you and your unco-operative trolley might stumble upon.

89

Deep End
Terri Pray

'I thought you just wanted to stick your toe in the water, Cathy?' Mags's hand tightened on her arm.

Cathy sighed and turned to look at her friend. 'Look, no one made you come with me. This was your choice, not mine.' Not that she regretted having a friend to lean on here but Mags didn't have to know that. Even she had to admit that the club was a bit on the wild side. With chains hanging from the black-painted walls, alcoves with St Andrew's crosses, whipping posts, spanking benches, and more, the place was more than she'd ever imagined possible.

'Why don't we go down town? There's a new club we could try, free drinks for women until midnight.' Mags leaned in a little closer. 'I don't like how they're looking at you.'

'You mean us.'

'No, you.' Mags insisted.

Cathy frowned but stopped and took a second look around, this time focusing on the men and women in the club. More than one gaze had turned her way and the intensity in their looks all but stripped what little clothing she was wearing from her body.

'Perhaps you should have worn something a little different?' Mags whispered.

Cathy looked down, flushed, and then lifted her chin. 'I figured this would help me fit in.' OK, so perhaps the short black miniskirt, stockings, heels, black bustier and a little black velvet choker hadn't been the wisest set of choices.

'Come on, please. Let's get out of here before ...' Mags pleaded and took a step toward the door.

'Before what?'

'Before something stupid happens.'

Her jaw set and she turned, slowly removing Mags's hand from her arm. 'Like what?'

'I don't know, maybe before one of those leather-wearing weirdos comes over here.'

'Maybe that's what I want.' She lifted her head up and cast a long, slow, sensual smile at the men and women who glanced her way. 'I came here for something and I'm not going to leave before I'm ready to. If you want to go, then fine, I'll manage on my own. Not like anyone's going to try and force me. You saw the rules when we walked in. We had to sign off on them, remember?'

'Like that will protect us if they try something. I'm not buying it and I'm not staying.' Mags stepped away, shaking her head. 'You can come with me, or not, but I can't handle this place.'

'I'm staying.'

Mags opened her mouth to say something and then shook her head, turned and left, one hand raised in a backward wave.

'Shit,' Cathy muttered under her breath. She hadn't actually expected her friend to go through with her threat. She took a step, and then two, half wanting to follow Mags out through the door, but then stopped. No, she'd come this far and she wasn't going to back out now. If she did, there'd be no second chances, no coming back to try again.

It was now or never.

'All alone?' A deep, rich male voice spoke behind her.

She turned, her breath hitching in the back of her throat. She swallowed hard, trying to put her thoughts in order before she answered. 'Yes.'

'A crime.' He didn't touch her. He didn't even take a step toward her, but she could feel the passage of his gaze over her body, taking in every inch of who she was. 'First time here?'

'That obvious?' Her cheeks burned and she shifted her weight from one foot to the other.

'To me, yes. The gear gives it away. You're trying too

hard.' He gave her another long, slow look. 'But it looks good on you.'

'Thank you.' She lowered her gaze for a moment, but when it rested on the outline of his semi-erect cock against his pants, she quickly lifted it again.

'See something you like?' He grinned, a dark light dancing within his gaze.

'Sorry, I didn't mean to look.'

'Ah, and you avoided my question. No matter, you'll tell me eventually.'

'I'm Cathy.'

'A pleasure.' He smiled and took a step toward her. 'So, why here?'

'I'm curious, I guess.' Wasn't he going to mention his name? 'OK, who are you?'

'Drake.'

'Is that a real name?' The words escaped before she could stop them. 'Sorry, I didn't mean it that way. It's just I've never met anyone called Drake before.'

'It's a scene name. Most of us use them. You might want to think about choosing one for yourself if you plan on visiting places like this on a regular basis. Unless, of course, you'd like your dominant to choose one for you?'

'My dominant?' She shook her head trying to avoid his gaze. There was something about the way he looked at her. Her skin tightened beneath his gaze, nipples pebbling under the black leather bustier. Her heart raced and a deep-seated warmth built between her thighs. 'I don't have one.'

He jerked his head at the surroundings. 'And yet this lot hasn't scared you off the way it did your friend.'

'No, why would it?'

'Newbies can be easily scared. But let's test how interested you really are.' He moved in closer, settling one arm around her waist, his grip firm but not painful as he walked her away from the bar towards one of the alcoves where a small group of people had gathered.

Cathy tensed but didn't fight him. The gathering had spiked her curiosity and the small sounds that reached her ears before they found a space where she could see, only added to her interest.

Heat flushed across her cheeks and she didn't know where to look when Drake stood her in front of him so she'd have a clear view. There, in the middle of the alcove, was a spanking bench with a nearly naked woman tied over it, bottom up, exposed for all the world to see, except for a thin strip of material between her buttocks that had to be a thong.

'Oh ...'

'See something you like?' He leaned in close, encircling her waist from behind with one hand.

'I – I don't know.' She swallowed hard. 'Why are you holding me like that?'

'Don't you like it?' He slid his hand up, cupping the underside of her breast. 'Or is this better?'

This was going a bit fast. She opened her mouth to protest, to tell him to move his damned hand. But her body had another idea. 'Better.'

'Good girl.'

Cathy sucked in her lower lip, chewing on it nervously. The woman on the bench wasn't alone. A man stood at her side, stroking her back and talking to her in a low-pitched voice.

'She wants this? I mean, with everyone watching?'

'She's fully consented to it.' He thumbed her nipple through the leather.

Cathy shivered, her nipple hard and aching beneath his touch. Some of what he said made sense, that it was consensual, yet even though he'd given her the choice in being touched there'd been an edge to his voice. Something that made it clear if she'd said no, he'd have turned away and found someone else to spend the evening with.

'Just watch what happens with the girl and then you can decide if you want to stay or if you'd be best following your friend to a tamer establishment.'

'OK.' She turned her attention to the submissive on the spanking bench.

The man had moved so he stood at the side of the bound submissive, a paddle in his hand. He didn't speak but brought the paddle down hard and fast against the woman's backside. Her soft cry filled the air and her bottom tinged red before the second blow landed on her upturned ass. A third and fourth followed without granting the bound woman time to recover. By the tenth, the woman was sobbing but her hips rolled and the scent of her arousal was strong.

'Well?' He whispered against her ear.

She whimpered, a deep tremble running through her body. Each time the paddle struck the woman's bottom Cathy's inner walls clenched. How could she tell him what she was feeling?

His fingers closed on her nipple through the leather bustier. 'I asked you a question.'

The paddle smacked once more and Cathy's hips rolled.

'A verbal answer, girl.' He pinched sharply.

She hissed between clenched teeth but the pain did something she hadn't expected. The pain formed a line between her nipple and her clit. Both throbbed. One in pain the other with a burning pleasure. 'I – I don't have an answer.'

'Yes, you do. I don't tolerate lies, girl. Perhaps I should take you to one of the alcoves and punish you?'

Cathy shook her head. 'No. Please. I couldn't take it. All those people watching me, I mean.'

Drake pulled her back through the crowd away from

the scene in the alcove. 'But in private you're interested, is that it?'

'Yes, it's what I came here to explore.' There, she'd said it. 'And I know there's more to it than a simple paddling. If you thought that was going to frighten me off you were wrong. I've seen worse on the net.'

'Watching on the net isn't the same as real life.' He laughed, pulling her towards a door. 'But if you're serious I can help you explore, girl. I have a private play area here that I pay for every year.'

This was happening too fast. She couldn't do this. Or could she?

He stopped, away from the crowd, his gaze locked with hers, his voice a deep, seductive whisper. 'You want this; I can see it in your eyes. The question is will you let your fear get the better of you, or will you submit to your own desires?'

She glanced back at the crowd and then looked at Drake. She licked her lips nervously. 'How do I know you won't push beyond my limits?'

'If I ignore your safe word then you'll report me and I'll lose my access to the club. Not something I'd want to go through, especially as the club would then share my "lapse" with every other club they have contact with. That's how serious the situation would be for me.'

Was it enough? She'd read the rules, even signed them, but would they follow through with them? Yes, they had to.

'All right.'

'You consent?'

'Yes.' There was no going back now.

'Good.' He took hold of her left arm and courteously led her to a set of double doors. The doors were locked with access granted by a keypad and Drake quickly punched in a set of numbers. The light on the pad turned from red to green and the click that marked the doors unlocking was audible even with the background noise of the club.

Once they were past the doors, and they had closed behind them, the noise faded into the background. A single flight of stairs took them to the next floor and three doors down Drake used a keycard to gain access to a room. He leaned in and flicked on the light before opening the door fully to allow her to enter the room.

She almost changed her mind when she saw what the room contained.

A large bedlike platform dominated the centre of the room, although there was a St Andrew's cross on the wall, and several floggers, canes, and crops hung from hooks close by. Cuffs connected by chains were attached to both the platform and the cross but she didn't see the rest until she stepped into the room. On the wall nearest the door hung hoods, blindfolds, and gags, and she couldn't help but wonder what lay within the chest of drawers on the left wall.

The door closed behind her with a solid thunk.

'If you need to leave and I, for whatever reason, won't let you, then you hit the panic button there.' He gestured to a large red button close to the bed platform. 'All the private rooms have them in case of medical or other emergencies.' He moved toward the centre of the room. 'Your safe word is Red. Understand?'

'Safe word? Oh, erm, the word I say to stop everything, right?'

'Yes.' He took a step toward her. 'Now, strip.'

'What?' She paled instantly.

'Unless you want me to cut off your clothing when I have you restrained. We are alone, girl. No one else is going to see you.' He didn't move, but stood there watching her. 'Are you going to obey me, girl?'

Cathy reached for the ties on her bustier and began to work them free. She was doing this. She was actually going to let someone dom her! What was he going to do? Spank her? Use a cane or flogger on her? Was she ready for all of that?

She folded up the bustier and set it on top of the dresser. The skirt followed it, leaving her standing there in stockings, heels and panties. Her left hand drifted upward, covering her breasts, though he'd already had an eyeful.

'And the rest.'

'I thought ... well the girl still wore panties for her spanking.'

'And this is private. No one else will be able to see you except me. You either strip or leave.' His gaze narrowed cold and dark as he looked at her. 'Well, girl, what's your decision?'

She glanced at the door and then back at him. 'But why do you …?'

'This isn't open for discussion.' His voice was ice cold.

Her breathing hitched in the back of her throat. 'OK, I'll do it. I just need a minute to …'

'Now.'

Her hands moved before she realized what she was doing. She hooked her thumbs into the sides of her panties and skimmed them down her thighs. The thin strip of hair over the curve of her mound brought a flush to her face.

'Better. You can leave the stockings and heels on. I've relented a little. You won't be completely naked.'

Somehow that didn't make her feel any better.

'The cross or the bed? The cross, I think.' He gestured toward the St Andrew's cross against the wall.

The cross held less fear for her than the bed but walking to it took more strength than she'd ever believed possible. Her palms were damp but her heart raced and her nipples were hard and aching for his touch. A liquid heat coated her nether lips and her clit throbbed. What was she doing? There was enough time to change her mind – there had to be. And he'd given her a safe word that would end things if she didn't like what he was doing.

'Reach your hands up, girl.'

She looked up and to each side before she lifted her hands up to the edges of the frame where manacles waited for her wrists. Would it hurt, being bound like this?

Drake locked her wrists in place. 'Now your legs. Ease your left out toward the manacle.' He knelt down by her left leg and soon both of her legs were locked in place. 'Good, now we can begin.'

'What are you going to do?'

'Sir ...'

'I don't understand.' She frowned and twisted to look back at him over her shoulder.

'Face the wall.' He touched the back of her head. 'And you will address me as *sir* during our little exploration. Is that clear?'

'Y–yes, sir.' She looked at the wall and shuddered.

'Better, much better.' He traced one hand slowly down the length of her spine then reached between her thighs and cupped her naked nether lips. 'You're already wet, girl.'

'Yes, sir.' She blushed at his words but there was no denying the truth. Her body hungered for something she couldn't express. She was wet for a man she didn't know, a stranger who hadn't even told her his real name.

'Good.' He moved his hand from between her thighs and cupped her left ass cheek. It lifted away from her flesh briefly, only to be brought down against her bare backside in a stinging slap.

She cried out, arching onto her toes, her thighs already stretched by the manacles. It hurt but the sensation between her thighs was intense. Her inner walls clenched, her body arching, lifting and offering her bottom to him again.

'Good, very good,' he growled in pleasure. He brought his hand down twice more before shifting to her other ass cheek.

She sobbed for breath, her hips rolling with each blow. Her thighs clenched, muscles taut as she tried to lean into his touch. This was happening too fast but her body welcomed it and needed what he was doing to her. 'More please, sir. More!'

'Greedy slut.' He laughed and stepped away, returning a moment later. 'But more you shall have. I like to see a girl enjoying herself.' He rubbed something over her backside. 'This is a paddle. Let's see if you like this the way you do my hand.'

Paddle? She tensed, remembering the paddle she'd seen in the other man's hand. How could he think she'd be ready for this?

The paddle smacked against her ass, harder, deeper than a blow from a hand. She cried out, shaking her head, wanting to deny him but it was too late. A second blow landed, harder than the first. She struggled against the manacles, her body pressed tight against the frame. The third one tore a wild scream from her lips.

'You can stop this with a single word.' He smoothed the wooden paddle over her stinging backside. 'You know that.'

She gulped, the pain easing to a deep warmth. Her pussy clenched, released and clenched again, seeking something, anything that would fill her. Her hips rolled now that he'd stopped using the paddle on her.

'You're horny. I can smell it. The scent of your pussy is everywhere.' He eased the edge of the paddle between her thighs. 'But this is only the beginning. There's so much more to introduce you to, slut. Are you ready for more?'

'Yes, sir.' She sobbed the words out. 'Please. I want more, sir.' It was more than a want. A need. One that threatened to burn out of control.

'Then more you shall have.' He moved the paddle between her thighs until the edge touched her swollen nether lips. 'As much as you can handle.'

And how much would that be?

The paddle moved swiftly, the edge slapping her pussy lips once, twice, three times, pulling soft hisses of pain from her. Then it was moved, down between her thighs, where Drake moved it, slapping the paddle from one inner thigh to the other and back again in rapid, sticking slaps.

She sobbed, twisting, moving with the blows. Blows that should have made her scream at him to stop, but she didn't. She only screamed.

'Do you want this to stop, girl?' He tapped lightly between her thighs with the paddle.

'No, sir. No I don't. Please, don't stop!' Had she actually said that?

The paddle picked up the pace, slapping harder and faster between her thighs. The pain radiated up into her pussy, vibrating in time to the slaps of the paddle.

'Are you sure?' He leaned in close, nipping the back of her neck, the paddle never ceasing its tapping torment. 'You screamed, little one. Screamed as if you were really in pain and afraid. Tell me to stop and I will.'

She whimpered, turning to look over her shoulder. 'Please, don't stop. I need more. I need …' Oh God, what did she need? This was all happening too fast! Her hips rolled, dancing with the tap of the paddle. She needed him, needed something, something she didn't dare name.

'You need to be fucked, don't you, slut?'

'Yes, oh God, yes.' She should have told him no. He didn't need to know what was going through her mind and yet she'd answered without hesitation.

'By me?' He reached up, tangling his free hand in her hair.

'Yes!' Why hadn't he gagged her? That way she wouldn't be saying such things.

'Then beg me to fuck you.'

'Please, sir, fuck me!' Why was she saying that?

He tossed the paddle aside. 'Is that what you really want, girl? To be fucked by a man, a dominant you don't know?'

'Yes, sir. I want … no, I need you to fuck me.' She squirmed as his hand cupped her heated mound.

He laughed, the sound cold and cruel, yet that only added to her need. She arched her back, pressing her bottom out to him. If he took her like this she couldn't stop him. She'd be helpless and taken at his mercy. It didn't matter that the reality was nothing like the fantasy her mind now offered her – that she could stop him with a single word if she desired.

In this moment she was helpless, about to be taken by a man she didn't know.

He moved his hand from between her thighs and stepped away. A ripping sound caught her attention and then a soft tap of something hitting the floor. She frowned, uncertain what she'd heard.

Something pressed between her thighs as he placed one hand on her hip, pulling her bottom out, away from the frame. The head of his cock pressed between her swollen nether lips, filling her pussy in one hard, full stroke.

Cathy sobbed in delight, her slick inner walls clenching around his cock. Her hips rolled, pushing back as far as she could when he pulled out, only to slam back into her. His balls slapped against her tender lips, his hand tight on her hip, controlling her body as he filled her again and again.

She groaned, welcoming each deep thrust even as his free hand reached around to touch her clit, his fingers searching, finding and circling the small throbbing nub. With each new thrust her body soared a little higher. There was something else, a sensation she hadn't counted on.

Clothing?

He was still fully dressed!

She wanted to be angry, to tell him to stop, but it felt right. This wasn't a lover's tryst, but a hard, fast fuck to satisfy an itch they both shared.

She wanted to move, to turn and see him, but she couldn't. The way she was bound on the frame meant she was being taken, not made love to. That should have turned her off, but it didn't. Instead she burned hotter, higher than she'd ever experienced before.

Each new touch to her clit was timed with a thrust. Her walls clenched, released and clenched again. A pressure built in the pit of her being and threatened to consume her. She cried out, sobbing, pleading wordlessly as her core wept, wanting him to take her harder, faster and deeper than before.

'You're going to come for me, but not yet.' He buried himself deep within her core and slowly licked the back of her neck. 'You're going to wait until I give you permission to come. Do you understand me, girl?'

'Yes, sir, I understand.' She shuddered, her body struggling to regain control of itself. Once he'd said the words her body had wanted to disobey him. She tried not to move or to think of the feel of his cock as it slid slowly in and out of her but it was impossible.

He tapped one finger against her clit. 'You want to come, don't you?'

'Yes,' she groaned.

'But you won't, not until I let you.' His finger moved rapidly on her clit.

'No, sir.' Her hips circled, her inner walls tight around his cock. She didn't know how long she could hold out. If he kept this up much longer her body would betray her, and then what?

'You know I'd punish you if you came without permission, don't you?'

'Yes, sir,' she whimpered, struggling to still her body. Her thighs tightened and her inner walls rippled along the length of his cock.

He pulled slowly out of her body until only the tip of his cock remained within her. The slow, deliberate movement tormented her inner walls as his finger did the same with her clit. His breath was hot and heavy against the back of her neck as he played with her body, forcing her to feel every small touch, each breath, scrape of skin against skin, even the feel of his clothing brushing her body.

She couldn't hold on any longer. 'Sir, please!'

He growled, thrusting into her hard, fast and deep. So hard that the St Andrew's cross groaned and the chains attached to the manacles rattled, but still he didn't give her permission to come.

Pressure built beyond control, her body aching, threatening to spin her into the void and yet still he forced her to endure more.

'Sir!' she pleaded.

His finger and thumb closed on her clit, pinching it. 'Come for me now!'

Pain and pleasure mixed in a wave that consumed her. She arched, her muscles clenching, hips writhing as she pressed back against him. He growled, thrusting, filling her, his teeth scraping against the back of her neck as he pushed her to the edge of sanity. Her ability to think fled. All she knew were the waves of pleasure that hit her one after the other until she no longer knew where one ended and the next began.

And then it was over.

With a low, sated groan he pulled free of her body, leaving her hanging in the manacles.

She'd done it, stuck her toe in the water, but in doing so she knew there was no going back to the life and the world she had known before tonight.

A stranger, this Drake, had shown her that this was where she belonged.

Hot and Bothered
Kat Black

Trapped inside the little timber-board beach villa, the night air is stifling. On the oversized honeymoon bed that dominates the shadowy, driftwood-chic interior I toss and turn, unable to sleep.

Briefly, I consider trying the old sheep-counting trick, perhaps swapping the traditional fluffy animals for the innumerable pillows stacked against the headboard; but settle for hurling most of them to the floor instead. Around my calves the sheet weighs as heavy as a woollen blanket and with a flurry of irritable kicks I work myself free.

Gaining no relief at all for my efforts, I huff and flop over onto my back, picking at the T-shirt plastered to my clammy curves. Glaring up through the dimness at the stationary blades of the fan suspended overhead, I wonder how much longer it can take to restore such a basic necessity as electricity to a luxury holiday resort.

As close and cloying as the humidity is, I have to admit it's only partly responsible for my state of restless insomnia. Squeezed in the grip of an intense nerve-fizzing, tooth-grinding sexual frustration, I'm way too wired to relax, let alone sleep.

Determined to at least try, I shut my eyes and block out any thoughts likely to further incite my riotous libido. I succeed for all of thirty seconds before my one-track mind is revisiting a sun-drenched beach full of taut, tanned torsos, glistening wet skin and contour-clinging trunks. The fidgeting threatens to start all over again.

Clapping one hand against the insistent niggle of need between my legs, I hold it down over the pyjama shorts covering my pubic mound and press hard. Beneath the pressure of my fingers, the fluttering pulse intensifies to a heavy throb and with a half-strangled sob I begin to rub against it.

If I thought the room was hot, it's nothing compared to the heat radiating through the flimsy cotton barrier of my shorts as they sink easily into the moist valley between my labia. With each circling pass of my fingertips, the roughened edge of the seam at the gusset catches the sensitive nub of my clit in a way that makes my breath hitch and my nipples twinge. I can't help but quicken the caress.

This is just what I need. Around and around the pleasure builds, the pressure tightens. Brushing my other hand across my chest, I feel the rigid pucker of my nipples pushing up against my T-shirt and use my nails to flick against each stiff little peak in turn, firing bolts of electric exhilaration back down to my groin. My spine bows off the mattress and my knees draw up, thighs squeezing together to lock my hand in place at their juncture ... I freeze as a soft mumble sounds from the pillow beside me. My eyes fly open.

Straining to listen over the pulse pounding in my ears, I lie there for interminable seconds, stiff as a board, still as a statue, mortified as a Catholic. Only when I hear a gentle snore and feel a wash of booze-scented breath drift across my face do I dare risk a peek out of the corner of my eye.

In the semi-darkness, I can just make out slack features and a gaping mouth, and with a sigh of relief I retract my fingers from their compromising location.

At least poor Sara has managed to find a state of blissful oblivion despite the unremitting temperature. If anyone needs the escape of sleep, she does. In the five emotionally raw days since she'd been left standing stricken at the alter by her louse of a groom she's seemed hell-bent on drowning her sorrows with the aid of every last drop of rum in the Caribbean.

And who can blame her? I lift my head to scoop my hair away from my perspiration-soaked neck and fan the damp tendrils across the pillow. When the jilted bride had insisted on going ahead with the week's luxury honeymoon, substituting me – her redundant maid of honour – for said missing groom, I'd let her hysteria override my concerns that a romantic couples' destination would be the type of place more likely to rub salt into her gaping wounds than provide a pampering salve to her torn and broken heart.

If either of us had known quite how sensual the ambience of Eros Cove was going to be, how beautifully and relentlessly seductive the setting, I'm sure we'd have reconsidered in favour of a loud, purgative, girls-behaving-badly weekend clubbing in Brighton instead.

Shifting onto my right side, I pound the pillow into a more comfortable shape and remind myself of the futility of *if onlys*. For better or worse, here we are; the decidedly odd couple out in a dreamy, magical lovers' paradise of sun and sea and sex and sand. No wonder Sara's being driven to drink and I'm being driven to distraction.

And then there are the men! I doubt I've ever seen a finer collection anywhere in my life, strutting their stuff across the tinted mini-screens of my sunglasses by day, only to keep my mind on continuous spool half the night. Figures all the good ones would be here in a couples' resort: tantalising, tempting and taken.

Even more frustrating is the sure knowledge that everyone in the place is busy getting their rocks off as and when they want. I flip over onto my left side and shut my eyes, wondering what I wouldn't give to join their ranks and to be lying here right now, naked, legs draped over a broad set of sun-burnished shoulders, ripe pink flesh laid open by firm, tanned fingers in welcome of a hungry mouth and a scruff-roughened jaw. Or perhaps sweat-soaked and pinned to the mattress by a smooth, hard body rocking the impressive length of an equally smooth, hard cock into my quivering depths with rhythmic control.

Oh, yeah. After several particularly dry months in the expanding desert of my love life, I could just imagine how good that wet glide would feel as it stretched and invaded, raking my neglected nerve endings with pleasure over and over and over again.

With a gasp, my eyes spring open and I finally admit defeat, giving up any thoughts of sleep. Between my legs, my shorts are damp with more than just perspiration, and the throb of desire is worse than ever, demanding that I take matters into my own hands, *now*. I'm too paranoid to risk the shared bed again, and the idea of creeping into the pitch-black bathroom to administer a bit of furtive self-pleasuring while my friend snores nearby just doesn't seem very pleasurable at all. Maybe I should try and cool things down instead.

Sitting up, I slip over the side of the bed. Moonlight shines in through the angled slats of the window shutters, striping the pillow-scattered floorboards and illuminating my path towards the door.

Even as I pull it open, I can feel it's a degree or two cooler outside than in. Grabbing up my room key, I step out onto the veranda and close the door behind me.

An idyllic vista of white sand beach and glassy, silver-hued sea stretches in front of the villa, framed by tall palm trees. Tiny waves froth at the shoreline, benign and inviting, making my toes wriggle at the prospect of a refreshing dip. I'm tempted, but with the cautionary echoes of the music from *Jaws* playing in my head, I find myself lured by the appeal of the swimming pool instead.

Half expecting to find the fantastical watery playground full of other overheated, sleepless guests, I'm pleasantly surprised to discover no other signs of life in, on, or around the interconnecting assortment of lagoons, tributaries, mini-islands and bridges.

Ignoring the signs telling me the pool is closed after midnight, I wander over a bridge and onto one of the islands where I come across a semi-secluded grotto constructed of natural rock at the end of a shallow inlet. With no light other than the diffused glow of the moon, I figure it's a dim enough hideaway to conceal my rebellious presence.

Lowering myself onto a large flat rock overhanging the water's edge, I dangle my legs into the crystal-clear pool. A sigh of bliss escapes as I trace swirling figures of eight with my feet. Placing the room key beside me, I gather up my hair, using the band kept around my wrist to secure it in a loose knot at the back of my head.

The air hitting the damp skin of my nape makes it prickle and itch as it begins to dry. I dip a hand in the water and raise it to smear the area with soothing moisture, repeating the action until the drips accumulate and run down my neck and shoulders to sneak into the top of my T-shirt. Like a teasing lover's touch, the rivulets trickle down my back and chest, working their way south via meandering paths that leave me shivering in their wake.

After the next dip, I let my hand hover above my legs, first one and then the other, enjoying the sensation of the droplets splattering onto my skin and drizzling down over the ultra-sensitive zone of my inner thighs. Inside, I feel an echoing ooze, warm and sweet and slow as honey. So much for cooling things down.

By now my shorts are well and truly wet through, and with a flash of recklessness and a careful scan of the area to check I'm still alone, I tug the soggy things down over my thighs, lifting one leg at a time to pull them off. It's naughty and liberating to feel the warm stone against the bare flesh of my rump and I dare to spread my thighs, letting the night air brush its breath onto the humid cleft of my nether lips.

The sensation is delightful but nowhere near enough. Dipping a hand into the water again, I use the other to bunch my T-shirt up against my stomach before bracing it behind me. Leaning my torso back, I employ the hover technique again, letting water drip from my fingers down through the trimmed triangle of my pubic hair, feeling the skin beneath twitch at the sensation.

Drip, drip, drip; the droplets gather together and snake their way down into the slick ridges and valleys of my folds, searching out tickling paths of least resistance. It's not long before I'm breathing hard and my arse is squirming against the rock. I need more.

Lowering my hand, I have to bite back a moan at the touch of my water-cooled fingertip brushing against the tender pearl of my clit. Spreading my legs wide, I tilt my pelvis up and trace my middle finger down to the opening of my vagina. Circling around the entrance, I coat it with my own slickness before returning it to stroke over the swollen nub in a satiny glide. Back and forth, round and round, I touch myself as fizzing streamers of delight unfurl from that one spot, shooting tremors out to my nerve endings.

A sound of movement from the pool terrace sends my heart leaping into my throat. Whipping my head around, I'm horrified to find a uniformed security guard patrolling into view. The beam of his torch sweeps within metres of my location, and splayed and vulnerable as my position is, I dare not move. Like a rabbit caught in the headlights, I sit frozen and wait for the inevitable to happen.

I can hardly believe my luck as, with a swing of

his torch, the guard veers off in another direction, the bobbing light disappearing down one of the paths winding through the lush gardens. I don't realise I've been holding my breath until it escapes in an explosive rush. In the aftermath of all the adrenaline flooding my bloodstream, my fingertips and toes begin to tingle.

That had been close! Not to mention frustrating. I'm more ramped up and in need of relief than ever. Perhaps the option of the hot, dark bathroom isn't so bad after all. At least it's private.

Grabbing hold of my shorts and room key, I push to my feet, standing in the knee-deep shallows of the inlet and giving my wobbly legs a moment to steady before turning to step up onto the ledge.

'No, don't go.' The low appeal sounds from somewhere close by, startling a yelp from my throat and spinning me around so fast I'm on the verge of losing my balance and toppling into the water. Throwing my weight in the opposite direction, I end up planting my arse back on the rock with a loud stinging slap. Clapping both hands over the juncture of my thighs, I use the screwed up bundle of my shorts to hide my nakedness.

'It's OK. Don't panic, I work here.' The voice sounds again as my wild-eyed search picks out a dark shape detaching itself from the shadows beneath the bridge opposite and gliding through the water out into the moonlight. 'I didn't mean to scare you.'

Is the jerk kidding? He nearly killed me! My poor heart is bursting inside my chest. It can't take much more of this kind of treatment, I'm sure. Shaking with shock and all but hyperventilating, I sit there and stare dumbly at him, wondering what – if anything – he's seen, yet dreading to even contemplate the answer. I hope the semi-darkness disguises the telltale burn of guilt blossoming across my cheeks.

'The guard's gone,' the pool-lurker observes in what I begin to register as a west coast American accent. With a wary eye, I check him out as he wades closer through the chest-deep water. From the sun-streaked, shaggy tousle of hair brushing the bronzed width of his shoulders, to the carved talisman hanging from the leather thong around his neck, and the swirling wave tattoo banding the biceps of one arm, he certainly has more than a whiff of LA surfer dude about him. Not least the laid-back smile he flashes as he adds: 'Stay, please ... at least until you get to finish what you started.'

Horrified, I gasp, remembering just in time not to throw my hands up to cover my flaming face in shame. A rush of denials, excuses and accusations tumble over each other to be the first off my tongue. 'You were watching me?' is all I manage to blurt.

'I was,' he admits in an appreciative tone, moving slowly but steadily nearer. 'Watching ...' His teeth flash white as his smile stretches wider. 'Wanting ...'

I didn't think I could blush any harder, but I'm wrong.
'I'm, ah …' Well, I'm at a total loss for words, actually.
Easiest to go with the facts. 'I … I don't know what to
say.'

'Then don't say anything,' he says with playful
simplicity. His open uninhibited approach and relaxed
manner are a million miles away from the gauche, nervous
wreck of an impression I'm making of myself. 'And don't
look so ashamed. You looked amazing touching yourself
like that. So hot all I can think about is touching you too.'

My overworked heart tries to jump out of my chest
again, but this time every thud is amplified by an echoing
beat in my groin. I don't know what my body's getting so
excited about; as attractive as the prospect might seem,
it's not like I'm going to let anything happen with a
total stranger, even one I do sort of recognise as a hottie
instructor from the watersports shack on the beach. 'Um,
I'd really better be going.' Easier said than done, I realise,
as I'm still clutching my shorts in my hands instead of
wearing them.

The stranger continues his gliding advance. 'You got
someone waiting for you somewhere?'

Of course! Sara the Snorer is the perfect excuse to get
me out of here. So why do I sabotage myself by saying
'Ah, no. Not really'?

'Me neither.' He grins and, reaching the shallows,
surges to his full height.

119

I gasp at the sudden rush of movement that leaves him standing only shin-deep, water sluicing down the lines of a body that is sculpted, lean ... and totally naked. Not an arm's length from my face, an admirable erection juts, hard and thick and long. My pop-eyed stare is captivated by the elegant up-curve of the shaft and the flared definition of the broad head.

Dripping rivulets of water run down the proud column, heading for the pair of tight, round balls framed by the sopping nest of curls between his thighs. Behind my teeth, my tongue tingles, thirsty to lap up every last drop.

It's only when I hear a chuckle that I realise I'm gawping shamelessly. My gaze snaps up to see that smile beaming down at me. 'So you'll stay and play?'

Hormones raging, brain spinning, I can't seem to form a single rational thought. What should be a case of clear-cut refusal is instead clouded and confused by lust.

'Unhf ...' is all I manage to articulate.

The laughing, wet dream of a vision in front of me comes closer and hunkers down to level his face with mine. 'You British are so cryptic. I'm hoping that translates to yes?'

'Um.' God, up close he's beyond gorgeous: all sparkly eyes, dimples and cheeky confidence. Surely I've just dreamt up such perfection? 'I don't think ...'

'Good. Thinking gets in the way,' he says, eyes twinkling attractively into mine. 'What really matters is that the two of us are here … alone.' He drops his voice and reaches down to pull one of my hands away from my groin. 'And we both want the same thing.'

His touch is cool and wet and gentle against my skin as he unfurls my clenched fist and raises it to his mouth. Keeping our gazes locked, he closes his lips around the fingers I'd been touching myself with, tasting me with obvious relish.

'Oh!' I gasp at the unexpected feel and intensity of the sensation. 'Oh, Jesus, what's that?' Whatever's going on inside his mouth it's like a sizzling current charging from the nerve endings in my fingertips directly to my nipples and clit.

Amused by the strength of my reaction, he pulls my fingers free and raises his brows in question. 'This?' He sticks his tongue out to show me the silver barbell pierced through its centre. 'You never had a lover with a tongue bar?'

I shake my head, struck dumb and numb as my imagination runs riot, chasing down all the exquisite possibilities presented by that magical silver ball.

Looking pleased, he leans in close. 'Then you're in for some fun.' His tongue is a brush of warm velvet as it licks the parted seam of my lips and takes advantage of my gasp to slip into my mouth.

The first thing to hit me is the taste of hot-blooded male, potent and intoxicating as dark rum. Next comes the strange new fascination with that tongue bar as the balls tap gently against my teeth, probe the roof of my mouth and glide over my curious tongue. Then, lagging behind in third place, is my conscience.

A small voice of sanity demands to know what the hell I think I'm playing at with this guy. *Push him away*, it bleats, as his hands move to rest on my tightly clenched thighs. *Tell him to get lost*, it insists when those hands caress and coax my legs apart. *Slap his impudent face and run*, comes the desperate cry as he shifts his body into the v-shaped space, bare skin wet and warm where it brushes against mine. *Do it now! Before it's too late!*

But swept away by the sensual onslaught of licks and sucks and swirls, I can barely bring myself to hear the thoughts let alone co-ordinate and carry out the actions. As my pool man's lips leave mine and his attention starts to move south, I know it's already too late. All I can think about is the devastating potential of that silver ball and how badly I want to feel it on me.

Taking my hands, he positions them palm-down on the rock to either side of my hips, then slides his own palms up the insides of my thighs, pushing my legs wider as he lowers his face between them. This should be where I pull away, where I baulk at sharing my most intimate secrets with a complete stranger. But caught up in the thrill of the unknown, it's surprisingly easy to remain still

122

and let his fingers split apart the plump lips of my labia, exposing the tender pink flesh hidden inside.

I watch, transfixed and tremulous, as he pauses mere inches from his destination to look his fill and breathe in the ripe scent of my desire. A low hum of pleasure sounds in his throat, and when his gaze finds mine again he smiles and treats me to a wicked flash of his tongue bar. 'Breathe,' he reminds me before burying his open mouth between my thighs.

Oh. My. Fucking. Heavens. Wet heat meets wet heat and delicate flesh yields to the uncompromising pressure of that silver ball. What a thing of torturous beauty the contrast is. The intensity is more than I can bear. Lurching forward, both hands fly to push his head away, but my fingers are prised from his scalp with easy strength, my hands guided back behind me and held locked into place. Trapping my squirming legs between arms and ribcage he takes full advantage, flicking that ball against the nub of my clitoris and making me buck and whimper. I come in less than a minute, shuddering from head to toe.

He doesn't stop after my first orgasm, but rather tightens his grip and ups the ante, sucking hard and fast on my still-throbbing clit then tapping the ball against it to bring a second barrelling on the heels of the first. Holding me open he makes me ride it out until I'm left mewling and swaying.

When I think my body's been squeezed of every last

drop of pleasure, he releases one of my wrists and pushes two fingers deep in the snug channel of my vagina. I can feel how slippery I am in there, can hear my juices squelching around every delving thrust. With curling strokes he finds my G-spot and at the same time flattens his tongue to rub the ball firmly against my over-sensitised flesh. I only realise that my eyes are closed when I see lights flash against the insides of my lids. From a long way off I hear myself begging him to stop even as I grind myself against his mouth and splinter apart for a third time.

Eventually, he raises his head and grins. 'Told you.'

'God!' I rasp in a shaky voice. 'Do you have a licence for that thing?'

'No, ma'am. Unfortunately, I don't have a condom either.' Rising, he shifts to sit on the rock ledge beside me, splashing a good deal of water about. Reclining back on his elbows, he lets his thighs fall open. 'So I hope you won't mind returning the favour?' He nods to his bobbing, dripping erection that looks fit to burst.

He doesn't need to ask twice. 'With pleasure,' I say, reaching to wrap one fist around the base of his shaft, and leaning over to swallow him straight down. Underlying the surface coating of cool, chlorinated water is the more fundamental taste of hot, horny male.

I might not be able to offer the benefits of a tongue bar, but I've never had a problem making good use of the oral attributes I was born with. I set about sampling and probing and savouring the intimate briny tastes of my sexy, sun-shiny surfer boy until every long, lean muscle in his body is trembling with tension.

It's not long before I feel his shaft pulse and swell against my tongue, and with a curse and jerk his hands are on my head, forcing me up. His cock pops free of the suction of my lips just as creamy strings of semen begin spurting from the head, arching through the air before landing across his clenched thighs and contracted abs.

Gasping, he collapses back onto the rock in a boneless sprawl. 'Goddam, that was good.'

Gasping, I hide my face in my hands as reality comes crashing back, and with it, shame and doubt. 'I can't believe I just did that.'

'Uh-oh.' I hear him shift beside me, still huffing and puffing. 'Guess I didn't do the job quite right, huh?'

Confused, I risk a peek at him from beneath my fingers. 'What do you mean?'

He peels my hands away from my hot face. 'I mean, you shouldn't be able to think straight enough to be worrying right now.' Sliding one hand behind my neck, he slips the other under the hem of my T-shirt. 'That's an oversight I'm gonna need to fix.'

Using his weight, he bears me down onto my back, pushing my top up as we go. 'Now, what's that term you Brits like to use? Oh, yeah, "just lie back and think of England."' He smiles and waggles his tongue piercing at me.

But right now I can't think of anything except the feel of his mouth closing around my nipple.

Supply and Demand
Elizabeth Coldwell

The blinds are drawn; jasmine-scented candles burn on the nightstand, casting a soft glow over the bed. Within easy reach, I have a glass of crisp, chilled Chablis, a bottle of raspberry-flavoured lube and my favourite anthology of bondage-themed short stories, dog-eared from repeated reading, should I need a little extra help in getting turned on – though I can't see that being necessary tonight. Squeezed onto a more than usually packed commuter train on the way home, I found myself squashed up against a broad expanse of chest belonging to a red-haired student type, sweetly geeky behind black-framed glasses. The enforced body contact – and the rather large bulge in his khaki shorts, the one he was so desperate to pretend didn't really exist – kept me on a rolling boil all the way home, and now I finally have the opportunity to do something about it.

Closing my eyes, I slip into fantasy land. I'm back on that crowded train, pressed tight against Geek Boy, and I snake a hand down into the tiny gap between our bodies, to loose his cock, long and thickly veined, from the fly of his shorts. The breath catches in his throat as I start to stroke him. Alarm that someone might notice what we're doing gives way to rising desire, and he jerks his hips as much as the confined space allows, pushing his shaft deeper into the grip of my steadily wanking fingers.

I roll a finger over my clit and feel the tight little bead respond to my touch, sending quivers of sensation through my belly. It's good, and I could play with myself like this for a while, lost in a delightfully rude daydream and making the slow ascent to my peak. But already I'm desperate for more, aware of an emptiness in my pussy that needs to be filled. My faithful vibrator lies on the bedcover, loaded with fresh batteries and ready to go. Grabbing it, I twist the base and set it humming into life, spreading my legs wide so I can slide those eight fat inches of purple plastic between my juicy lips.

Which is the exact moment the phone rings. If I ignore it, whoever's calling will go away, I tell myself, trying not to lose the erotic mood I've worked so hard to create. But they're persistent, and I'm forced to concede defeat. Tossing the buzzing vibrator aside, I pick up the phone and flip the cover open.

'Hello?'

'Marissa. How are you, darling?'

'Mitchell. I'm fine. What can I do for you?' Of all the people I wanted to interrupt me at a time like this, my ex-husband would be way down at the bottom of the list. Oh, as divorced couples go, our relationship is on the cordial side – we've always tried to adhere to the maxim that you should love your child more than you hate your ex – but even so, he's caught me mid-wank, and I can't help feeling resentful, particularly as he's the one with a new wife and a baby on the way, and I'm the one lying alone on my bed, fantasising over some random guy I rubbed up against in the rush hour.

'I hate to ask, but I need you to do me an enormous favour. It's parents' evening at Lily's school tonight.'

Trying to turn the vibrator off discreetly, so he won't hear the telltale noise in the background and realise what I've been up to, I do my best to keep the irritation out of my tone. 'Yes, of course, I hadn't forgotten. But why are you reminding me? You know the arrangement. You attend parents' evenings; I go to the end-of-term play. You take part in the dad's race at sports day; I provide cakes for the bake sale. Or do you want to change the terms of our agreement?'

'Not at all,' he assures me, 'but we've had a major power outage in the office, and all the servers have gone down. There's no way I'm going to be able to get away from here until we've fixed the problem. To be honest, it could take hours. So, just this once, could you go down to the school for me, please? I'll make it up to you, I promise.'

I want to say no, and go back to my wine and my book of naughty bondage stories, but I have to be more mature than that. After all, how long can it take the teacher to tell me that, yet again, Lily's up at the top of her class and absolutely no trouble at all? But I'll have to get a move on. Already it's gone seven, and the parents' evening finishes at eight. 'OK,' I tell him. 'I'm on my way. But you owe me a box of those champagne truffles I like. You know, the ones they sell at the chocolatier on the high street.'

'Sure thing. Thanks, Marissa.'

With that, he's gone. Taking a hefty gulp of my wine to fortify myself for what's to come, I slip into my skirt, struggling to zip it up as I hunt round for the shoes I kicked off on the way into the bedroom. My panties are nowhere to be seen, and I'm running so late I don't have time to fetch another pair from my underwear drawer. Looks like I'll be turning up to parents' evening bare beneath my respectable work suit, but what does that matter? After all, who else but me will ever know?

* * *

It's a brisk twenty-minute walk to St Susan's Junior and Infant School, a journey I used to make twice a day when we still all lived together as a family. When I arrive, cars are parked on the playground, but already the flow of traffic is away from the school, rather than towards it. Walking through the main door, I'm immediately hit by a smell that makes me nostalgic for my own schooldays, a mixture of chalk and floor polish, with a faint undertone of damp PE kit.

Lily's form room is at the far end of the school, through the main hall, with its proud displays of pupils' artwork, from the splodgy handprints of the reception class to the papier-mâché stegosaurus produced by the top year juniors. I pause for a moment outside the headteacher's room, outside which stands a trophy cabinet containing all the prizes handed out on school sports day, and a small fish tank filled with darting cichlids and neon tetras. Checking my reflection in the glass door of the trophy cabinet, I run a hand through my windblown curls. Then I pass on, to Room 10, where Lily's teacher waits.

At first, I think I've made a mistake. Sitting behind the desk is not Mrs Shenton, the grey-haired, mumsy woman who's been teaching Lily for the past year. Instead, I'm greeted by the sight of a man who can't be any older than twenty-five, with dark fashionably tufty hair, a stubbly growth of beard and biceps that bulge beneath the sleeves of his black T-shirt. My pussy, deprived of a much-needed orgasm by Mitchell's unexpected phone call, twitches back to life at the sight of him.

'Excuse me, this is the Year Six classroom?' I hover close to the door, ready to back out if I'm in the wrong place. 'Only I was looking for Mrs Shenton?'

'Yes, that's right, but she's off with glandular fever at the moment.' He beckons me to step forwards and take a seat on the other side of his desk. 'I'm Jake Greening, the supply teacher who's looking after her class till she gets back. You did get the note explaining the arrangements, right?'

I shake my head, flustered by being in the presence of this unexpectedly hot man. Vaguely, I recall Lily mentioning something about another teacher, but all the official paperwork goes to Mitchell, and he'd neglected to fill me in on the details. Still, there's a vague kind of symmetry to the situation: me, the stand-in parent, dealing with him, the stand-in teacher. 'I'm sorry. That would have been sent to my ex-husband. And he's the one who should have been here tonight, but there's been an emergency.'

'Oh, you don't have to explain to me, Mrs–' He runs a finger down his list of names and finds the one pupil whose parents haven't made an appearance yet tonight. 'Mrs Durham.'

'Call me Marissa, please. Mrs Durham is married to my ex.' I grin. 'I'm sorry. I'm probably making this more complicated than it needs to be.'

'No, that's fine. I might not have been in the profession

132

long, but I've learnt plenty about the mysteries of extended families. Anyway, it's nice to meet you, Marissa.'

Jake holds out a hand for me to shake. When I do, his nose wrinkles and he looks at me oddly. He can't detect wine on my breath, surely? I made sure to crunch a couple of peppermints on the way over; an old trick, but one that usually works. Then the truth dawns. In my hurry to leave, I neglected to wash my hands. The scent of my pussy must still be on my fingers.

Blushing, wondering what kind of slut he must think I am, I mutter, 'So how is Lily doing this term?'

'Oh, what can I say about Lily?' It's the same line Mitchell and I have heard from her teachers almost since the moment Lily toddled into nursery school. As he talks me through her progress in the various subjects, praising her for her consistently high marks and excellent attendance record, I can't prevent myself from tuning out. My mind returns to my earlier fantasy of wanking off a guy while we're pressed close together on a train, surrounded by a mass of oblivious commuters. Only now, the man whose cock is hot and pulsing gently in my grasp is no longer that sexy red-haired geek. It's Jake.

My thighs rub together, sticky-wet, as I shift in my seat, consumed with thoughts of bringing this gorgeous supply teacher to the stage where he's gasping against my shoulder, only a few sly strokes from shooting his come over my fist.

'… when she moves up to senior school next year. So, do you have any questions?'

With a start, I realise Jake is looking at me, having finished his spiel and clearly expecting a response. Does he know I haven't paid attention to a thing he's said, too busy admiring the full pout of his mouth to actually follow the words it's been shaping?

'No, I think that's everything. Thanks so much.' I rise from the low chair, all too aware of my pantiless state and the juices pooling in my sex. If anything, I need to come more urgently than I have at any point since I started my journey home tonight. What, I wonder, would be the etiquette on finding the nearest toilet cubicle, locking myself inside and bringing myself off on school property?

Fortunately, Jake spares me that dilemma. He shuffles all his papers into a manila folder, fixing me with his soft brown gaze. 'I don't want to sound like I'm coming on to you or anything, but I'm finished for the evening now, and I haven't made any plans for later. So – would you like to have a drink with me?'

Despite his protestations, to my ears it sounds exactly as though he's coming on to me in his understated, polite fashion, and I welcome the approach, pleased to learn my strong attraction to him isn't one-sided. It's exactly how the evening should progress: a couple of drinks, some idle conversation, a game of footsie beneath the table. Call it a token attempt to get to know each other just a little better before we head for the bedroom. But that all takes time. Time I don't have right now. He can't possibly be aware of it, but at this moment I don't care that Jake is a virtual stranger, a good ten years my junior and charged with the responsibility of educating my daughter. All I can think of is how badly I need to be fucked by him.

'A drink would be nice, Jake, but there's something I'd like even better first,' I purr. I know I sound like the worst type of cougar, hunting down her young prey without mercy, but I can't help myself. 'Is there anywhere we can go where we can have a little privacy?'

The cutest of flushes rises to his cheeks at my blatant propositioning of him. Seems he has just a touch of the shy geek lurking below the surface, revealed in his suddenly awkward manner. An undeniable weakness on my part, it's what first attracted me to Mitchell. Yes, I have a type, and Jake fits it to a T.

But despite my overpowering eagerness, he doesn't tell me to slow down or back off. Instead, he thinks for a moment, then says, 'I know just the place.'

Taking my hand, he leads me to the little stock cupboard, its door tucked away in the corner of the classroom. When he opens it, I find myself confronted with an Aladdin's cave of teaching aids and toys: wire baskets full of soft balls and plastic bats; squeezy bottles of poster paints in every shade of the rainbow; boxes of pencils and chalk and hard rubber erasers. An empty hamster cage and a half-full bag of straw bedding take up most of the free space on the floor. With everything that's crammed inside, there's only just enough room for two bodies to squeeze in close together. So different to my fantasy of sex on a busy train, but still with the same sense of confinement and limited movement that made it so exciting.

'You're OK with this?' I ask him, not sure why I need to receive his spoken consent. He's certainly giving every physical indication of wanting this, if his dark, dilated pupils and the hard-on tenting out the fly of his jeans are any reliable indication.

He nods. Pressed tight up against him, I can smell the spicy cologne he favours, mingled with a hint of his own more intimate aroma. 'I've wanted you since the moment you walked into the classroom, Marissa. I just didn't think things would move quite so fast. But I don't have a problem with that, if you don't.'

I don't, and I prove it by rising on tiptoe to kiss him. Even in my heels, he's a good head taller than me, and he bends his head so our mouths meet, softly at first, then with growing urgency. My tongue traces the full contours of his lips, his stubble prickling at my cheeks. Jake's an assured kisser, giving the impression he'd be happy to explore my mouth for hours if I'd only let him, and my nipples peak stiffly against the cups of my bra.

Grinding myself onto his crotch, I hear his breathing quicken, and slip a hand down to cup the bulge that presses at his zip.

This is fun, but what really gave extra spice to my fantasy was the thought of having my lover unable to use his hands, letting me set the tempo as I played with him. There, it was easy to imagine him crushed into a tiny space in the carriage vestibule, pinned on both sides by strangers' bodies, but if I want to replicate that here, I'll have to find some other way.

Just in my eye line, at the side of Jake's head, there's a skipping rope, the soft length of white rope wrapped snugly round its two wooden handles for ease of storage. Snaking out a hand, I bring it down from the shelf. Eyes closed, lost in the feel of my lips nibbling at his, he doesn't realise what I'm doing till I've unwound the rope. Catching hold of his wrists, I push them together behind him. Though he's bigger and stronger than me, he doesn't attempt to resist. His eyes gleam with a strange excitement as I secure him in place with the rope, looping it around his wrists and tying him to the shelf. I have no great skill with knots, and I'm sure he could free himself without much effort, but I don't think he's even going to try. It seems Jakey-boy gets a thrill from being restrained. Of course, if we'd gone about our seduction in a more usual way, instead of cutting to the chase with a haste that made speed dating look like a long and stately courtship, I'd have discovered this about him, given enough time. As it is, we've reached the point where I have him bound and at my mercy by delicious serendipity, and I'm determined to make the most of my new-found knowledge.

'You like this, don't you?' I say, stroking his cock through his jeans once more. It's trapped within the denim, desperate to be free, but I don't pull his zip down just yet. I'm enjoying the way he bites his lip with frustration, pleading with his eyes for me to take him in hand.

'Like what?' he asks.

'Being tied up. Being in a position where I can do exactly what I want to you, and you can't do a thing about it.'

He doesn't deny it. 'So what are you going to do to me?'

Grinning, I tell him, 'Whatever I want.'

With that, I finally take pity on him, unzipping him and bringing out his cock. It's a nice size in my hand, as I wrap my fingers around it and begin to slide the velvet sleeve of skin back and forth over its plump head. He groans, and I realise I'm in danger of taking him too close, too soon.

Stepping away from him, I let my skirt fall to the floor. His eyes widen in surprise and delight at the sight of my pussy, unconstrained by underwear, slick and ready to be fucked.

There's a box containing building blocks tucked under

the bottom shelf. I pull it out and stand on it, bringing myself up to a point where my cunt is level with Jake's proudly jutting cock.

Clearly impressed by my resourcefulness, Jake sighs with pleasure as I guide his cockhead up between my lips, engulfing as much of his length as I can. Clinging tight to his neck, I urge him to fuck me. Then a second voice seems to join in the clamour.

It isn't my imagination. I can hear a voice calling Jake's name.

'Shit!' he exclaims, his voice cracking with the effort. 'It's the head. She must have seen the lights still on and realised I haven't left yet. If we keep quiet, I'm sure she'll go away.'

I fight not to make a sound, though I'm overcome with the urge to giggle. Of all the times for someone to come looking for him!

The door handle rattles, inches from my bare backside. 'Jake, are you in there?'

This is the moment everything goes horribly wrong, I just know it. Any second now, the head will burst through the stockroom door and find me half-naked, with Jake's hands fastened to the shelf behind him and his cock buried to the hilt in my slippery cunt. He'll probably get sacked on the spot, and as for me …

Yet, far from dampening our ardour, the imminent danger of discovery only serves to make me hornier. A small, shameful part of me actually wants her to catch us in the act.

Jake keeps his composure long enough to call out, 'Yeah, Wendy, I'm here. I'd let you in, but I'm a bit tied up with something at the moment.'

That's the moment when I almost lose it, and alert her with my screams of laughter to what's really happening in here, but somehow I keep myself under control as she replies, 'Well, see you tomorrow, bright and early.'

We hold our breath as the sound of her heels clacking against the parquet floor grows fainter. At last, there's only silence. 'That was close,' Jake murmurs.

'Don't worry about it. Just shut up and fuck me,' I order him.

He does, moving with all the freedom his bonds will allow. As soon as he starts to pump in and out of me, I know this will be quick, but I've been on the edge of climax for what seems like hours now, and it will take very little of this wonderful friction to tip me over. Speeding the process, I drop a finger down to the apex of my thighs, finding my clit and strumming it with precision.

Yelling out Jake's name, I surrender to the orgasm that tears through my body with such force I'm in danger of toppling off the box I stand on. My cunt clutches tight around his shaft, milking the spunk from him, and he slumps against the shelf, spent and panting.

'That was amazing,' I tell him, reaching round to untie

his wrists. We share soft, sloppy kisses, then reality hits us and we seem to become aware for the first time that we've just had sex in a tiny dark cupboard that smells of hamster bedding and Plasticine.

'Maybe now's a good time to go for that drink we were talking about,' I suggest, dressed once more and ready to leave. 'We could go to a pub if you want, but I've got a bottle of Chablis in the fridge, and I do hate drinking alone.'

Jake nods. 'Sounds good to me. Why don't you lead the way?'

The lights are on in the neighbouring classroom, a cleaner patiently mopping the floor. It's definitely time to go. Tomorrow, I'll ring Mitchell and let him know how the parents' evening went. Tonight, all I want to do is take Jake home and teach him more about what it takes to please me.

Here There Be Dragons
Chrissie Bentley

'Hey, Chrissie. Have you ever had a threesome?'

I'll say one thing for my friend Lisa: she always knows how to catch your attention.

'No, I can't say I have,' I started to say, but she was already chatting on.

'I've been thinking about that a lot just lately. I think it's something to do with the aging process.'

I eyed her curiously. 'It's not just because you can't keep your legs shut, then?'

'Seriously. Think about it, when you're young, everything's a brand new experience. But as you get older, haven't you noticed how your options just start drying up? You and Dave, for example. You've been together however long, a year or whatever, and I bet half the things you were doing when you first met have been completely forgotten about.'

'OK, you do have a point, there.'

'Right. And why is that? Because you know one another so well you've just settled into a routine. There's no time for play any more, no room for experiment. You just get in, get out and get on with your lives. Pete and I were exactly the same.'

'But that's not why you broke up.'

'I didn't say it was. What I am saying is, I've been thinking about how exciting sex was when we were younger and how I miss that thrill of discovery now that we're no longer young. Which got me thinking about things that I've never done and that got me thinking about threesomes.'

I smiled. 'Well, you got there in the end. You should go for it.'

'I'm going to. I was just wondering, who should we pick for our partner? It can't be anyone we know or who we're likely to see.'

I interrupted her. 'Hey, what's all this "we" business? When you said a threesome, I thought you meant you and two guys. Or, at least, some other couple.'

'God, no. What happens if I hate it? At least if you're there ...'

'I can take over?'

'No, I was thinking more along the lines of, you wouldn't be insulted if I don't want to ...' Again her voice trailed off and, for the first time in this entire conversation, it dawned on me that she was actually being serious about this. The question I now had to answer was, was I?

It's funny, but one of the first things out of any guy's mouth, once he's got you into bed, is 'Have you ever done it with another girl?' Beat him to it, ask him if he's ever done it with another guy, and he'll probably flip (unless, of course, he has), and start demanding to know if he comes across as gay. But not only are girls meant to take the question seriously, the big hope is, they'll answer yes. Well, sorry to disappoint you, fellas, but the closest I ever came was in high school, when I had a crush on a girl in my hockey team. Then it turned out that she felt the same way about me, and the romantic possibilities of the entire situation suddenly crumbled, never to be revisited again.

But, if I had to get it on with another girl (and, from the way Lisa was carrying on, it rather sounded like I might) she, Lisa, would probably be my first choice. At least we've known each other long enough that, if it should go wrong, there'd be no hard feelings. And if it goes right, then our friendship unfolds in a whole new dimension. It's a win-win situation and, if I keep on telling myself that, I might even come to believe it.

'OK, so how are we going to do this?' Lisa was asking. 'We don't want to go anyplace we know people or where word might get around – we do have our reputations to keep up, after all.'

I shot her a sidelong glance: as if she'd ever cared about that fragile commodity.

'Hey, I know, how about a weekend at the shore?'

I thought for a moment. 'That would work. Dave's working Sunday, and I think he's got some baseball game on Saturday, so we weren't planning on seeing each other. It'd work for me.'

'Me too. Look, I need to be getting back to work, but I'll check some hotels on the web when I get home, see what I can book us in to, then I'll give you a bell this evening and let you know what I've found. OK?'

'Great.'

She leaned forward and pecked the end of my nose. 'Cheer up, girlfriend, I might be all your Christmases rolled into one.'

'Yes.' I gave a mock pout. 'And you know how much I love Christmas.'

Back home that evening, I carried on wondering precisely what I'd gotten myself into, but had to admit I was curious as to where it might end up. Sitting on the bed, but still clothed, I began moving my hands across my belly, first imagining it was another woman's touch, then that it was another's flesh I was feeling beneath my T-shirt. I allowed a hand to stray up to my breast, squeezing and stroking it over my bra, homing in on the nipple and teasing it. At least I'll know where everything is, I thought to myself. It won't be like some guys' early attempts to hit the right spot on their partner. I let my other hand drift beneath my skirt and lightly stroke the gusset of my panties.

I was faintly surprised to feel it moistening and tried to concentrate my finger in my mind on her pussy. I felt my lips yielding slightly and increased the pressure of the single probing finger. Her finger, my pussy. I felt a light jangle in my clitoris, but ignored it for the moment, sweeping the tips of my fingers across my inner thighs, while massaging my breast even harder. I wondered if Lisa had already been through this routine herself, while she was making up her mind to ask me, and the thought excited me even more. My finger slid inside my panties and I pushed it deep, then began to bend and unbend it, massaging that magical patch that we're told is called the G-spot, but which I always think of as my private Eldorado, a place for which many men have searched in vain, but which I can locate with my eyes closed. OK, Lisa, you're on, I thought, then the phone rang and I snapped out of my passion-trance.

'Hotel Turquoise, Saturday. Check in at two, out at noon. How does that sound?'

'I'll see you there.' I hung up the phone, and sat without moving. Oh God, it's going to happen. It's really going to happen, I thought. Eldorado was forgotten. I was really going to do this.

* * *

And so it was, two days later, Lisa and I were sitting on the beach, planning our next move. And I'll say this for Lisa: she doesn't waste time. We'd only been on the sands half an hour and already she had three guys, in three different directions, eyeing us – or rather her.

'So, what do you think?' she asked, admiring her handiwork.

'OK, him.' I nodded towards the bronzed Adonis seated to our left. 'He's right out. He's way too proud of his bulges and lumps and he probably thinks sex is just another way of doing push-ups. The barely-out-of-his-teens looking kid with the radio blaring Van Halen has a friend with him and I am definitely not going there. Which leaves the one sitting with his face half-buried in a book and sneaking sweetly shy glances in our direction. So now what do we do?'

'Easy.' Lisa jumped up and crossed the few yards of sand to our target. I watched his eyes growing larger as she headed towards him, five foot six of well-proportioned blonde, with boobs to die for almost spilling out of her bikini top. She knelt on the sand and I watched them exchange a few words. Then she came back. Behind her, the guy was already gathering up his book, towel and backpack.

'I told him that Mr Muscles over there kept staring and was freaking us out and asked him if he could walk us to the boardwalk and, if we were attacked, he could run and get a cop.' The strange thing was, Mr Muscles was staring, or maybe it wasn't so strange, given that we'd obviously made our choice, and he wasn't it. I'd hate to be his gym equipment this evening.

By the time we got back to our hotel, everything was set up. Well, not absolutely everything, but at the least the groundwork had been prepared. Mark – an unmarried engineer in town for some kind of gaming convention – would meet us in the lobby that evening, for drinks and dinner and then on to a club. All the way up to our floor in the elevator, Lisa was hopping from one foot to the other, delightedly chanting, 'We've caught a nerd, we've caught a nerd.' Then, as though the thought had just occurred to her, she said, 'How ironic. He comes to town for a weekend of fantasy; that's what this gaming thing's all about, isn't it? Dungeons and Dragons and stuff? OK, he comes for one fantasy and he's about to fall into another one entirely. Oh sister, we are going to blow his tiny mind.'

'You're not planning to be mean to him, I hope?' I knew what Lisa could be like when she got into one of these moods, but she swore she'd be on her best behaviour.

'Not only that, but when we're finished with him, he can even stay and watch us.'

'Oh, I can hardly wait.' I hoped I didn't sound too sarcastic.

Mark, the nerd, arrived on time, bought our first drinks and would have happily paid for dinner if I hadn't

148

grabbed the check before he picked it up and told Lisa that she and I were splitting it between us. Of course Mark protested. I mollified him by letting him leave the tip, then Lisa kept me talking long enough that he paid for the three of us to get into the club. I really hoped she would keep her promise about behaving. I don't know what engineers earn as a rule but this was shaping up to be an expensive night out.

It was also beginning to look like a washout. Mark was nice enough but he had nothing to say beyond 'Oh, let me pay for that.' And trying to talk to him about anything at all, even Dungeons and Dragons, drew no more words from his mouth than the minimum required. I did learn that he wasn't into D&D and thought it was kids' stuff compared to some of the new games out there, but that was the extent of my conversation with him. Lisa was having even worse luck and, when she asked him if he wanted to dance, it was obvious that what she really wanted was someone to whisk her around the floor, so she could check out the rest of the talent in the room.

I sat back, watched for a while, then drifted to the bathroom. When I returned, the two of them were locked together in a kiss that had them rooted to the centre of the club as though the entire place was their own domain.

'Wow, what was that all about?' I asked Lisa when she finally returned to the table. 'And where's Luke Skywalker gone?'

149

'Hopefully to adjust himself.' She smiled. 'Listen, you might not believe this, but he has the most enormous chopper I've ever seen.'

'You've seen it?' I asked incredulously.

'OK, felt. We were dancing, right, and I could feel this … I guess you'd call it a mass … against my leg. So I was thinking he had something in his pocket, a bunch of old Kleenex maybe. And then it moved. I felt it move. And not just a little shift, this went from my hip down to halfway to my knee. And I thought, hello. I kissed him and it moved again. And, by the time I let him go, this thing was practically halfway up my stomach and as hard and hot as a witch's tit.'

I laughed, both at the expression and her curious simile. 'You sure you still want to share him?'

'That's the deal,' Lisa shot back. But, as we walked back to the hotel, Mark and Lisa arm in arm, and me trailing along a little behind them, I did begin to wonder. So, I think, did Mark, when we got up to our room and he noticed that both of us seemed to have a key. I saw his eyes flicker from Lisa to me and back again, and I tried to gauge his mood. Either he was asking, do I get you both? Or he was pleading, get her out of here.

My unbiased opinion? I think it was the first one. But Lisa had her own ideas.

'It's OK, Chrissie was going to take a long bath. Weren't you, Chrissie?'

The haste with which I answered yes suggested to me that I was glad of the fact that, no matter how excited either Lisa or I got over the thought of making love together, the reality was just a few steps too far. I closed the bathroom door, turned on the water and started undressing, then realised I'd left my book in the bedroom. I didn't know how long I was going to be exiled to the smallest room (till one of them needed to use it, I expect), but I wasn't going to spend the time staring at the walls.

In my bra and panties, I opened the door. I'd been out of the room maybe sixty seconds and at the very worst, I expected them to be sitting on the bed together, still locked in their pre-flight kisses. Instead, by the glow of a scarf-shrouded bedside lamp, I saw Mark flat on his back, his eyes tightly closed, and Lisa wrestling – yes, wrestling – to get her mouth around, indeed, the biggest cock I'd ever seen.

OK, I've been to the chat rooms, I've played the game, and when Longjohn14incher informs you that he's not called that for nothing, it's so easy to turn all demure and little girly and type back ooh I don't know how I'll ever fit my little mouth around that, but I'll certainly give it a try. And then you poke your pinkie between your lips and type a lascivious mmmmm.

It's not until you actually see fourteen inches, or as near to that as makes no difference, and watch someone

151

trying to accommodate them, that you realise just how absurd that kind of boasting is. That is not a penis. It's a lamppost and, with the best will in the world, would you really want one of them stuck inside you?

At the same time, though, it was fascinating to watch. Once, and only once, I let Dave set up the digital camera, and photograph me while I gave him head; and, though I deleted the pictures immediately afterwards, there was something beautiful about them, both the sight of his penis as it sank into my mouth, and the look of undiluted pleasure that danced on my face as I did so.

I saw that same kind of bliss in Lisa's face, but I also saw frustration, her eyes screwed up tight as her jaw strained around a purple mushroom the size of a fist. Her lips were drooling saliva all over it, desperately trying to get up the lubrication that would finally allow him to slip in all the way, but still the thick ridge at the bottom of the head was mashed against her lips, refusing to budge any further. It was almost painful to see and incredibly exciting. It wasn't until I felt my own wetness wash over my fingers that I realised that I'd even started diddling myself while I watched. The damp reminded me of my running bath, and I stepped back into the bathroom and turned off the taps. Then I resumed my position in the doorway, gently fingering myself as Lisa battled gamely on.

Neither of them heard me walk softly across the room

or noticed as I knelt down behind Lisa, my eyes now glued to the huge shaft with which she was fighting. Two hands held it, and the veins that stood out were as thick as her fingers. I manoeuvred myself around a little to study her lips as they sucked ferociously on what little of his manhood they had actually managed to seize upon, then I placed my hands on Lisa's shoulders, gently massaging them as she worked.

I felt her relax into my touch, the bobbing motion of her head slowing a little as I allowed my hands to slip over her shoulders, then back onto her shoulder blades. Mark groaned his appreciation of the change in pace, but remained motionless. Sensing that all Lisa needed was a little extra encouragement, I bent my head to kiss the nape of her neck, as my hand slid under her arm to clasp her breast and thrilled to feel her nipple digging hard into my palm.

I cupped her breast and squeezed, then allowed my fingers to roam to the corona, gently tracing patterns in the skin before lightly tapping the swollen bud. I found myself wishing Lisa had settled herself in a less constricted position; I yearned to fasten my lips around her nipple, to feel my tongue teasing its taut surface. Instead, withdrawing my hand for a moment, I slid my fingers into my pussy, then replaced them, slick and moist on her breast, and sensed from the tiny moan that escaped from deep within her throat that she knew precisely what I had done and was given fresh determination by it. With a sudden jerk, I watched astonished as her mouth finally closed over that leviathan tip, and began inching greedily down the shaft.

She would not get far; no girl could. But the extra purchase allowed her to remove one of her hands and, with a delighted shudder I had never anticipated, she clasped my hand that still massaged her breast and guided it slowly down towards her loins.

My fingers traced lines down her abdomen and belly, danced in the thick mat of her sticky pubic hair, then slid through a wetness that seemed to last forever. I curled my middle finger and sank it inside her, into an all-enveloping wetness that was as heart-stoppingly alien as it was deliciously familiar. Whenever I touched myself like this, the sensations were shared between my finger and vagina. Now it was my finger, fingers, as two more slipped in, that gloried in the hot wet softness, and I slipped towards her clitoris, rubbing and flicking it as her hips began swaying.

I could feel her orgasm building, her pussy muscles tightening, her juices flowing more fully; I could watch, as well, as the one hand that held Mark's penis became a blur of frantic motion. But it was jerking not towards bringing him to climax, but to the one which was now building closer and closer within her own frantic body.

For a moment I thought she was going to break the

thing. She was trying too hard. I moved away, watching as his cock hung in mid-air, a rigid bar that you could tow tractors with, then wrapped my hands around it as well, trying to slow Lisa's motions. It wasn't in the script, I knew, but drastic situations call for drastic responses.

I sucked a ball into my mouth – at least they were a reasonable size – then let my tongue drift towards his asshole, flicking the soft skin before tracing back across his scrotum to the base of his cock.

Suddenly, Lisa's head jerked back with an almost animal cry of ecstasy; at the same moment, precisely as his cock flew free of her mouth, an enormous fountain of come shot out of it, arcing over his body to splash down close to his shoulder. Sinking to her knees, her head on his leg, Lisa continued pumping him dry with one hand, producing pools that became great puddles of cream, spreading over his stomach and then trickling down his sides. But her eyes remained locked on my face, and her mouth – her poor, aching mouth – creased in a smile and a softly whispered thank you.

I smiled back, then placed my finger on my lips, pointed towards Mark, and crept back into the bathroom. As I closed the door and stood brushing my teeth and contemplating the now cold tub, I heard the bed creak as Mark sat up, and presumably opened his eyes at last. 'That was fantastic,' he said. 'But I really need to get going. I've got a game that starts at eight.' There was a thump as he swung his legs onto the floor, a swish and a zip as he pulled his trousers up, then a 'Bye. Er, thanks' as he walked out of the door.

Lisa had not said a word.

I opened the door and came out. 'Wow, are all your men that abrupt?' I asked, then stopped as she let out a gale of laughter, convulsing against the side of the bed and actually slapping the mattress as she tried to regain control.

'What's so funny? Apart from the fact that he'll never get laid with a monster like that.'

'It was ridiculous! You know, the first few minutes were fun, but, ow! I'm amazed I didn't get lockjaw. If you hadn't come along, I don't know what I'd have done.' She looked around the hotel room. 'Probably called room service and asked if they had a vacuum cleaner I could borrow.

'But this is the best bit. While we were walking back from the club, he asked, he actually asked if the three of us were going to do it together, and really coarsely as well, like "Is she your sister? Am I gonna fuck you both? Are you lezzies?" and how he couldn't wait to tell the others about how he just had his first threesome. All this shit, and I was like, fuck you, asshole, I'm going to get what I came for, which is that giant piece of meat you're packing, and then you're out of here. And then you coming in like that, and doing what you did ... don't

156

you see how perfect that is? I had a threesome, you had a threesome ... and he didn't know a single thing about it.'

She rose, went into the bathroom and I heard running water and the sound of her scrubbing her teeth. I climbed into my bed and picked up my book; moments later, Lisa was snuggling down alongside me, her arm warm across my stomach, her head nestled in my armpit. 'Please don't take this the wrong way ... I loved what you did, and I'll never forget it. But I really don't think I ...'

I kissed the top of her head. 'Don't worry, I don't think I can either.'

'Although there was a moment there when I'd have given anything to have been doing that to you, not him.'

'That,' I smiled, 'is your jawbone talking. Besides, if you had, you'd only be bitching about how sore your tongue is now. Some people are never satisfied.'

'Oh yes they are,' she whispered as her eyes closed. 'In fact, I haven't been this satisfied in months.' And then she fell asleep and left me wondering how I'd feel in the morning. Surprised that I'd done it? Embarrassed that I had? Or just plain furious that it never went any further? Well, I'd find out soon enough.

I Have You
Charlotte Stein

I don't react when he slides his hand down over my bare back. I'm used to not reacting. A hand can mean a million things, after all – a sign of solidarity, a touch of comfort, a suggestion that someone comes with you to the place you're meant to be going. And for a second I'm sure his hand is all three of these things together, because really it can't be anything else.

I don't know him, in that other way. The one where people tangle together and press their mouths to each other's and feel that thing ... What's it called again? Pleasure, I think it is, but pleasure is so far away from me it might as well be on Mars.

All I can do is dissect the various elements of his hand on my back: the way my skin almost seems to part beneath the press of his thumb. The way his knuckles feel when he turns his hand over and drags them down over me.

They feel heavy, I think. The backs of his hands are heavy, though I can't remember how I know this. When I close my eyes it's as though I can hardly picture his face, but then he leans in quite unexpectedly and touches his mouth to the nape of my neck and suddenly I can see it all clear.

He has brows that draw together too often, I'm sure, and eyes that are too often worried, and when the kiss on the back of my neck suddenly becomes hot and wet I think of his mouth. Soft, so soft, and promising so little.

But it promises a lot, here. I can hear him breathing in between those kisses, ragged and not quite in control of himself and, though such a thing should make me nervous, I find I feel nothing instead. Nothing at all, except for the minutiae of what being kissed is actually like.

I think I'm physically reacting to it, too. It's sort of like cracking through an ice-covered pond, only to find hot lava underneath. My skin catches fire, my heart starts pounding thickly, sluggishly – though it doesn't do so in my chest. It does so between my legs, where I'm somehow already wet even though this isn't anything at all, really.

I mean, it's rude that my back is bare. And though I've crossed my arms over my chest in a big X, my breasts are bare too. I somehow never got around to putting my top on, and so here I sit on my bed, staring out of the window over the windy rain-slicked hills, in just a skirt.

I must look like someone who's lost all of their sense of self. Like I'm vacant, though as soon as I think the word my mind changes it to *vacated*. I've been vacated. Something has left me and I'm just a limp thing staring at a grey world in half my clothes.

Aroused, but not really connected to my own arousal. In truth, I can hardly recall what arousal is – no more than I can remember the man behind me and his face of many parts – and I think so right up until he gets two hands on my hips and pushes me into a clumsy standing position, then begins ruffling up the skirt I don't remember putting on.

I think I know what he's going to do. It's obvious. But it's still something of a shock when I feel his mouth searching blindly between my legs – shoving me when he can't get at what he clearly needs to, the sounds he makes all desperate and somehow brutal at the same time.

My nipples are stiff, now. I don't even try to cover them. We're out in the middle of nowhere, but I suppose someone could walk by and see me like this – expressionless, trembling, my breasts exposed for anyone to look at. And yet I don't care. I don't care about anything.

And I have to confess, something about this intense sort of detachment excites me thoroughly. He's licking me in a really dirty way, now – right between the cheeks of my arse – but I don't give a damn. I just want to burn in that lava. I want to plunge right through the ice and boil alive.

I come close, when he slides two fingers into my cunt. Of course I'm sure it should hurt. The position I'm in isn't great – legs barely parted, stood as straight as an arrow – and I haven't been fucked in an age. I should be locked tight, resistant somehow.

And yet he just eases in as though I've turned to syrup, which I suppose in one way I have. I'm so wet I can feel it on my thighs, I can feel it sliding slickly around his fingers, and even if I couldn't I'd know about it because of him.

He makes a sound, a little moan of delight. My wetness stands in for my permission, and he fucks me roughly like that for a moment. Just in and out. Just good, firm thrusts that make me ache. And when I think I can't bear it any more, he slides his fingers through my slit – backwards, everything's backwards – and finds my embarrassingly swollen clit.

'You like it,' he says, in a tone that suggests he's surprised. And then with more assuredness: 'Oh yeah, you like it.'

Who am I to deny him? I *do* like it. He knows exactly how to touch me – two fingertips just rubbing over the underside of my clit, back and forth, back and forth like a metronome – and it isn't going to be long before I come.

In fact, I think it's going to happen in a short and rather humiliating amount of time. I've gone from trembling to shuddering and he keeps it up until I'm right on the

161

precipice. I'm just about to do it, I'm really so very, gloriously close, and then he quite suddenly removes his hand.

He bends me over at the waist, so that I'm almost leaning on the windowsill.

He won't actually fuck me, I think, frantically, but I'm wrong about that, too. I can feel something hot and smooth pressing between my legs, his hands on my thighs, urging and pushing them apart.

It's the only time the word *don't* swells up in my mind, like an ancient artefact of the forgotten me. The woman I was knew how to say no, to stand up, to ask and demand and negotiate. But I am not that woman any more. I am this limp thing, bent over, something hot and solid sliding into my body as though I'm just a receptacle.

Vacated, I think, and then he shoves into me again. Harder this time, but oh God, so much sweeter. I can hear him breathing again and this time it's really rough. It's bordering on a panting or a series of moans and I have to reach out and hold onto the windowsill just to keep myself steady. Just so that I have something to press my face against, the crook of my elbow, the soft turn of my forearm.

I think I bite myself, when the actual and real pleasure builds to some terrible point. I'm going to come, I'm certain, even though hardly anything has happened and I've no more memory of orgasms than I do of any other pleasant thing.

When it happens I'm still shocked. My entire body clenches against his now rapid and thrillingly forceful thrusts and I make a sound, a choking, half-sobbed sound, as my clit jerks and my cunt ripples around his cock.

When it's done I realise that I really did sob. When I reach up and touch my face, my cheeks are wet with tears that I don't remember crying.

* * *

The second time it happens I'm prepared. Or at least I think I am. I'm in the garden, fully dressed, so it's hard to really expect something like his hands on my breasts, through my shirt.

And he does it abruptly, too, like before. One second everything is normal: we're talking about the gardenias and the old elm we're stood by. Then the next he's undoing my shirt right out in the open, fingers fumbling with the buttons, alternating between getting the material off me and fondling my bare breasts.

Because of course I'm bare under the shirt. Maybe that's what caught his notice – the shape of me beneath the thin cotton. The stiffness of my nipples in the cold, February air. It had started to mist a bit, so maybe the material had grown a little see-through.

Now it's completely see-through because he's parted the two sides like wings, and before I can say or do anything he's kissing me there. He's kissing my breasts with that same hot, hungry mouth he had before.

I don't mind admitting that it feels good. I might have clung to some notion of restraint, before. Some remnant of what's proper and right, in these circumstances – with everything that's happened, you know – but I can't any longer.

He isn't holding back. He licks over my nipples in the rudest way a person can, and I can't help it. I have to bury my hands in his curly hair and hold tight to him as he does this to me. This thing, this thing – oh God, what is it again?

I don't know, but I moan to feel it.

I moan to feel him shoving my skirt up, hands too desperate again. Everything about this is rough and jagged, like the feel of the tree bark pressing into my back. He's going to take me against it, I think, but I don't fully understand that concept until he does it.

There's too much to process. The way his cock feels, thrusting deeply inside me. His hair still in my hands and the smell of him when I press my face to the side of his neck, like soap and some distant memory I don't want to unearth.

I come embarrassingly quickly this time. So quickly I don't even have a chance to think about it. The whole thing just swells up inside me and pours right out of my mouth in a way I didn't let it before.

164

'Oh just like that, yeah, like that, baby, do it, do it,' I tell him. And then there is a whole host of pleasure sounds. Moans and groans and gasps of delight, as I do my best to work the last of it out on his still-solid cock.

Of course he slows, as soon as I'm done. And then after a brief second to catch his breath he steps away from me. Buttons his trousers around his erection, tidies himself as though nothing happened. Like before, when I came around from the tears and the trembling to discover that he hadn't finished but had left the scene of the crime anyway.

Though it's obvious why, I wish it wasn't. I wish, I wish, I wish.

But it remains so, all the same.

* * *

I don't give him the chance this time. To surprise me, I mean. I strip off all my clothes, instead, and rather than waiting with my back turned I stand in the bedroom completely naked. I face him when he walks through the door.

He looks surprised, the way I have felt surprised. Though I don't think the two feelings are the same thing. One stems from the sight of me, so freely bared. The other is from the sense of some awakening, some pleasure I never thought I'd experience again.

'Rebecca,' he says, and his voice sounds so old and rusty. I think it's because I can't recall the last time he said my name. I'd started to think he'd forgotten it, but I can forgive him because I had forgotten his too.

I remember it now. It's hard to go to him and kiss him the way I used to. We used to tumble on to any available surface, tearing at each other's clothes, hands so full of each other it felt like greed. But now I'm just so broken apart, I'm that ice, melted and shattered and torn up. And though the heat is back there's still a flood of pain, too, when I kiss him.

I take off his clothes, one item at a time. He lets me do it in the exact same way I let him do those things for me, only this time I won't let it be detached, closed off, like a separate part of ourselves. I make him look me in the eye. I make him kiss me even though I can taste salt in his mouth and he's shaking.

He's shaking the way I was, when he kissed my back and made me take that pleasure. He made me. I want to make him.

'Rebecca, I –' he starts, but I put a hand over his mouth. I tell him *don't*, the way I probably should have by the window. But I didn't, and now we're almost back to life. We're almost there.

I don't regret it. I can't feel bad about wanting him. And I don't think he feels bad, not exactly. He only holds out for a moment or two and then suddenly he's pulling at his own clothes. His arms go around my middle and our naked bodies touch all the way down from chest to ankles, legs tangling briefly. The bed is waiting for us to spread ourselves all over it.

I can feel how hard he is against my belly but it's more than that. His teeth sink into my shoulder, his hands make bruises on my hips. And in return I give him as many marks, biting in places where I know it will show, then licking over every little sore spot I make.

He used to love that. He loves it still. Before I've even gotten halfway down his body he's moaning my name, hands in my mess of hair, hips rocking up against nothing. Just as he's at that perfectly lost place, gaze untroubled, brow unrumpled, I take his thick cock into my mouth and suck so hard.

Hard enough to make him gasp in a way that almost seems pained. Hard enough to make him thrust up and beg for more.

'Like this?' I ask. I drag my teeth over the length of his prick, before ending on the most lascivious lick I can manage.

His head goes back against the pillow. He's so close that I could tug him over the edge with just a little more. Clearly he hasn't allowed himself to do anything beyond the things he's done to me. He hasn't given himself up to it, the way I did. And though I want him to there's something I need a little more.

When he's just at that point of mindlessness, bucking and moaning and covering his eyes, I stalk up the bed and cover his body with mine.

It isn't difficult to take him inside me. I think he tries to stop me about halfway through, just as I ease myself down, hands on his shoulders, body thrumming with that new sort of heat. But when I lean over and kiss him he can't seem to hold onto that note of protest. His eyes stay open and on me, so blue and startling it seems insane that I had forgotten.

I'd forgotten what it was like to be gazed at. To be filled and fucked by him, slow at first but then faster, hotter. I twist above him, leaning back until I get that sweet pressure I crave, and when it comes it's like nothing else in the world.

'Oh God, Rebecca, don't,' he says, and I suppose he does because I'm really taking it now. I'm working myself on his cock, hips jerking, that pleasure cresting so swift and sharp I know I should be ashamed.

But I can't be, and he shouldn't be. He shouldn't be full of don'ts, I shouldn't be full of don'ts: we've had too many already and they've taken us to pieces. Don't be happy, don't carry on, don't live your lives the way you did before.

'I'm going to,' I tell him. 'I will.'

And then he puts his head back again for me, back arching, and I know he's doing the thing he couldn't before. He's coming inside me, hard and almost vicious, fingers digging into my sides as the pleasure pours out of him and into me.

Because that's what it feels like. It's like he's releasing something through me, and the moment he does I shake with that same blissful sensation. Cunt clenching hard around his cock, my orgasm like a tight fist unfurling in my belly.

It's unbelievable. I'm sobbing with it, again – only this time it's the good sort of sob. It feels like a relief, when I spread myself over him. And when he wraps his arms around me, I can feel his relief too.

'I didn't know if it was okay to love you like this any more,' he says, and his voice is so raw. It wasn't even like this on the day she died, which I suppose should make me feel worse somehow. But it doesn't.

I feel light, suddenly, as though a wound has been lanced and everything heavy in it flowed out of me the moment he spoke.

'It's OK,' I tell him. 'It's OK now. We still have each other.'

And we do. We do. I remember his name. I remember his face. He's not a stranger to me any more, just another ghost floating through the life we thought we'd have with our daughter.

He's real again to me. He's mine. My husband.

'We still have each other,' he echoes, and as he does

he cups my face in his hands. Lifts me from the crook of his shoulder so that he can see me. I think he sees me. I don't think it's just her hair and her eyes, any more – I think I'm me again.

'You don't have to be afraid, you know,' I say. 'If we had another it's –'

He shakes his head. Cuts me off.

'I'm not afraid,' he tells me. 'I have you.'